VIA Folios 177

Eleison

Published by Bordighera Press, an imprint of the John D. Calandra Italian American Institute of Queens College, The City University of New York.

25 West 43rd Street, 17th Floor, New York, NY 10036

Library of Congress Control Number: XXX

Cover image by Laurette Folk.

VIA Folios 177
ISBN 978-1-59954-227-0

ELEISON

Laurette Folk

BORDIGHERA PRESS

For my mother

TABLE OF CONTENTS

CHAPTER 1

HUMILITY SPEAKS FIRST

DANTE, 1989

Dante Alighieri Russo enjoyed the touch of his wife's hands as they rubbed the lukewarm cloth around his face; his skin was still tan from playing golf in the summer and the stubble at his chin provided a thick friction. He saw her fingers up close now, bent and gnarled like the branches of apple trees. He felt consoled by his wife's touch and wanted her to stay, but he knew she had to keep busy. There was this moment, however, when they looked at each other through Florence's hands. She smiled softly, tenderly.

"What?" she asked.

"The cloth feels good on my face," he said.

Florence picked up the bowl of soapy warm water and the cloth and left the room, and Dante focused on the red stretch pants that fitted to the curves of her body. She still had a fine rear end, despite her age, was still a good-looking woman, and he knew there would be others, joked about them, how they'd be knocking on the door while he was still warm in the grave.

Across the street, bells rang, and he heard the front door shut and Florence go to mass. St. Anthony of Padua Church was composed of granite with white marble pillars; its rock was something of greatness, intimidating. The gilded bird at its center altar was different from the common sparrows that swooped up and down from Dante's gutters, making nests that always clogged the waterway and drowned their young. The church was a place intricately involved in their everyday lives and major events—baptisms, weddings, even the funeral of his son, and eventually his own impending funeral—but it was not a place in which he felt comfortable. He was wary of the priests, men who forsook women for God, and he found the Sunday masses dull, impersonal, and rigid. However, the church, just a foundation when they moved in some 42 years ago, was the deciding factor to impel Florence out of Queens and away from the city—a means for cutting the cord between his burgeoning family and the greater tribe who had their own ideas of how Dante and his family should live their lives.

Lying in bed for days on end, Dante had become sensitive to sunlight, could tell when the sun ducked behind a cloud. The early morning light was diffused at first, gentle, hesitant; time passed and it poured in through the bedroom window spectacularly, spilling over the rumpled covers, illuminating the mound where the beast manifested itself in a 20-centimeter tumor on his bladder. As a butcher, Dante knew what to do with a knife, and he thought if he had the right one, he could cut the devil out, succeed in doing what the doctors couldn't. This was the thought in the back of his mind as he lay on his deathbed, an image of the sharp blade cleaving the grip where the beast latched on.

There were the cracks radiating across the ceiling that he never got around to patching, the closet door off its tracking from just a month ago by his overly aggressive motion to get it to move, the empty perfume bottles that Florence kept because she liked the elegant shapes, the beaded cross above the bed that they bought in Jerusalem, and the ghosts that came and went in the misty, faded glass of the dresser mirror.

The bedroom set was an Italian Chippendale Venetian Baroque with carved decorations of jesters and urns and flowers in solid walnut. It was a magnificent set, and it was the first item Dante bought when they moved in. Over the years, the mirror above the dresser had collected dust between the reflective layer and the glass, and it looked to the viewer as if his reflection was in the clouds, ethereal and unworldly. Dante thought of replacing the mirror, but Florence said she really didn't mind; it had an antique feel to it that she liked. Now, it seemed especially fitting in his last days, as a portal to the past and a means to reconcile with certain troubling aspects of his life.

Meryl was the first one to appear. The mists parted enough to show her red lips first, then her overly tweezed eyebrows, and then her worried eyes. He closed his eyes, tried to sleep, but he couldn't and his gaze returned to the mirror to watch it slowly unveil the ebony of her hair, how she moved around her apartment in hurried and intentional steps.

He had thought about her over the years, not because he loved her, but because she was associated with his greatest sin. Dante knew her from the bus stop in front of the store where he worked as a butcher some fifty years ago in Great Neck. Sometimes when he went to sweep the front mat, she talked to him. He thought she might have been a woman with a reputation, but she was not brash, was somewhat soft, despite her eyes, which seemed to be made of glass. It happened the day after Dante's son was born dead. He went to work, but closed the store early and walked to a nearby park where he sat on a bench feeding pigeons with stale breadcrumbs from his pocket. Meryl, returning home from her waitressing shift, saw Dante and stopped.

"Who turned you loose for the day?" she quipped.

Sensing that he wasn't in the mood for banter, she sat down next to him. He stared at the pigeons blankly. They sat for a while, not speaking, until she insisted that they go to her apartment for a cup of coffee.

She lived under the El; the scenery from her only window was a bridge abutment with the word SEX written in red on the concrete. Dante wondered who would write such a word and how they managed to do it in such a precarious place. The two-room apartment smelled of cigarettes, the only amenities a toaster and a coffee pot, an old stove with crumbs and caked-on spills. There was a Siamese cat; Meryl picked it up and brought it to her face for a kiss.

"This is Herman," she said.

"I hate cats," Dante said.

The train went rumbling by and Meryl lit the stove while Herman wove himself between her ankles, as if the entire place wasn't shaking and might come down, rain shattered glass onto the dresser. The gas didn't light, she cussed, took out a match and the burner popped with blue flame. She grabbed a can of coffee from the cabinet, Dante looked at her rump, it was flat, lifeless. She dismissed herself for a moment and disappeared into the bedroom as Herman approached Dante, jumped on his lap. Dante instinctively grabbed the cat and threw it so that it hit the wall, landed on its feet and let out a long hiss. Meryl rushed back in and looked at Herman.

"What happened?"

"I don't think he likes me," Dante said.

She sat down, lit a cigarette while the coffee perked and Dante thought of the child and his wet black hair and how he fit squarely in the palm of his hand. He remembered praying for God to open his eyes, praying for the boy to make a move, indicating that the doctor had it wrong, but the baby was terribly motionless and Dante could feel the warmth of his tiny body dissipating from his hand. He thought of the lock at the bedroom door; how he put it there to keep the kids from coming in whenever they wanted, but now Florence used it to keep him out.

"Maybe you should take some time off," Meryl said. "Maybe you are working too hard. All that driving back and forth to the Island."

Dante shook his head. "I'll just think."

They sat for a while, Meryl smoking, Dante thinking, and tolerating the El as it rambled by and shook up the place. She rose, poured the coffee into a cup. She took a milk bottle from the fridge and scooped out the cream and placed it in another cup, offered the sugar bowl with hard lumps Dante had to chisel apart to get a decent spoonful.

"I don't really drink coffee," Meryl said. "It upsets my stomach."

Meryl sat with her glossy eyes focused on him, coating her cigarette with lipstick to match the others in the tray. He was the one in mourning, yet he felt pity for her, for who she was. Where was her father to help her out? Where was her family? Could someone be this alone? He couldn't help himself, "What the hell are you doing in a dump like this?" he asked.

Meryl sucked on her cigarette. She was used to sentences like that and they began not to faze her.

"This is the way the meek live, Dante."

"Isn't there a girlfriend you could live with? A relative?"

"I'm fine where I am."

Meryl blew the smoke up to the ceiling. Dante watched it tumble down the sides of the mirror. The coffee was weak and tasteless, the large lump of sugar undissolved on the bottom of the cup. Meryl was trying to be a friend; the thought softened his heart. But it was getting late now, approaching dinnertime; Florence would wonder, would call the store. He looked at his watch, drank the rest of his coffee and stood up; in the face of the meek, someone had to claim strength. He went to the door and she followed him; when he turned around, she was right behind him, her eyes wide with apprehension. She was like a child now, wondering what he was going to do, if he would leave her just like that. Dante looked down at her, put his big hand across her throat, to keep her from coming any closer. He had the strength to strangle her, put her out of her misery. He looked at the cat under the bed with its wicked eyes. Dante's big hand formed a cup and his thumb touched the red of Meryl's lip.

Lying in Meryl's bed he watched the cat staring at the pigeons on the abutment of the bridge, its tail sweeping back and forth across the windowsill, like a pendulum on a clock keeping time. There was a streetlight illuminating the pigeons as they huddled together in their nests, vile things made of straw and shit. Dante wondered if the cat knew how to kill; if the knowledge was innate and despite all the years of domestication, would still surface if it was given the chance. He thought that it would. He rose, grabbed his pants and left the room feeling vacant, shameful; evil had its way with him and stole from him every last respectable thought and feeling.

It was his greatest sin, but it was too easy to call it that. Why did he do it? Because he needed a distraction from his grief? To get back at his wife for her years of blind submission and because she withheld her true self from him? She had completely shut the doors on her own desire; it was as if her spirit had flown somewhere else during their intimacy and he was left a body with which he could do whatever he liked. Dante often wondered, given his wife's obvious pious ways—mass every day, rosary beads between her fingers every morning, the 5-feet by 8-feet tapestry of the Last Supper in the dining room—if she were better suited for the religious life. But he never had the desire to be with other women, and Florence's aloofness, her mystery, piqued his desire for her all the more; it had always been this way, right from the beginning, when he repeatedly asked her out and she repeatedly refused until finally, fate intervened.

When Dante went to work for his uncle in the Great Neck store, he was seventeen. He was precocious for his age, responsible, and it wasn't long before he was managing the store with a thriving business. Most of his patrons were women, and women liked Dante because of his stature, his hands, his smell, the way he charmed them with wit, the way he called them "Sweetie" and convinced them he would do anything for them. Florence's mother, Philomena was one of his faithful customers, a stocky Italian woman who talked his ear off about the old country, who pointed and laughed and broke into Italian in bursts that shook the walls and caused the children to cower. Dante liked Philomena because she reminded him of his own mother, because she was filled with life. Philomena's husband was a tailor, fond of his wine and his daughters who worked for him as seamstresses in his shop in the city. When Philomena sent Florence to the store to get the week's meat, Dante fell in love with her. Florence had a face like Greta Garbo, and a one dimple smile, as if she were hiding things and she alone knew where they were.

Dante and Florence became engaged, and then Dante was called to duty overseas, made a sergeant and manager of a mess hall, because he could cook and he knew how to tell people what to do. The war made Florence a late bride. They married in the year 1945, had a daughter, Carmen, and when Dante returned, lived with the rest of Dante's family in a big apartment building in Ozone Park where everyone crowded around the one television in the building to watch the evening news. Dante was wakened nightly by his brother-in-law Tony's snoring shaking his bed posts and never had time alone with his wife and child, due to continuous visitors, Joyce to chat up

Florence about her broken heart, or Mary to complain about Tony, or Joe to ask for money to pay a bookie, or his father to bother him about joining the racket.

The mists in the mirror became smoke again, stifling, coalescing smoke that Dante could taste in the air. The men sat in his father's bar in Queens playing cards. Big Cheech said, "What do you want to spend your life carving up cows for?" Johnny the Shark pulled his father aside and told him what a fine son he had. His father kowtowed to them, let them stay past closing, laughing, spilling drinks, burning holes in the wood grain of the bar with the butts of their cigars.

"You could be better than everybody else," his father said.

"I don't like the way they do things," Dante said.

After his second daughter Nicoletta was born, Dante moved his family to the Island, to be rid of all of them.

Dante tried to adjust himself under the weight of the tumor. He thought of his wife and the many nights she shifted restlessly beside him in the later months of her pregnancies, how uncomfortable she was, how she only fell asleep sitting up, after hours of adjusting. He lay awake watching her peacefully doze in the moonlight, while his mind whittled away at the serenity with all that could go wrong, if she would go into labor while he was at work, who would be around to take her to the hospital, if the baby would be normal when it came out. He heard the door open and shut downstairs and it jostled him out of his thoughts. Florence came in and her cheeks were flushed. "I'll need to throw more salt on the steps before Bardo arrives tonight," she said. She fixed her hair in the faded glass of the mirror, looked at her husband through the mists, as he lay propped up in the bed. "I should help you to adjust, Dante, so the sores don't come back."

"It's okay. I think I'm okay," he said.

"Do you think you can eat? I'll make you a shake. It would be good for you to have something in your stomach to take the medication."

"Okay."

She left the room. The wind blew hard outside and he felt chilled; the windows he had put in last fall were not properly containing the drafts, as the contractor had promised. The old house could become unbearably cold; he remembered how one winter he chopped up all of the patio furniture and burned it in the fireplace for heat to keep his family warm when the temperature dropped below zero for a week. Dante was relieved when he heard the radiator hiss; he felt the heat coming into the room as the old radiator clanged and whistled. It was a sound that set him at ease, the sound of the house doing what it was supposed to do, without him lifting a finger.

The second ghost that appeared in the mists of the glass was a young priest. He could make out the shape of the priest's head, slightly bowed, his hands folded over his cassock. Through a hole in the screen, they looked long and slender, like a woman's hands. Dante recognized the priest immediately, the one he and Florence referred to as "the young one"; he had recently joined the parish and the other priests were old and gray and were there for decades. He was clearly an effeminate man, and Dante recalled men like him in the war, and the rumors and gossip associated with them, the neatness of their quarters, how they kept their appearance. He had told Florence about his suspicion and Florence scoffed, told him to get over himself, that he should get to know someone before he made a comment like that. But there, in the confessional, was the priest he thought queer and Dante immediately regretted his decision to confess his greatest sin, and wanted to leave. He panicked, debated what to do. The priest made the sign of the cross, whispering the names of the Holy Trinity as a hint and to start the confession. Dante resigned himself and sat down, feeling trapped. He said, "Bless me father, for I have sinned. It has been many years since my last confession."

"What is it that troubles you?" the priest asked.

"The devil," Dante said.

The priest sighed, as if he heard it all a thousand times. "How so?" he asked.

"I tried not to pay him mind. I raised a family. I worked hard. But now things are dull."

"Idleness," the priest said.

"Yes, idleness," Dante said.

They sat for a while without saying anything. Dante grappled with how he would broach the subject about the sin. All these years it was there, like a splinter that was never properly extracted, and now that he was getting older, it should be confessed, before something should happen and it was too late.

"There is a memory. I can't get over it."

The priest cleared his throat, as if he was about to speak, but then didn't.

"My wife—I love her. But there was this one time—. I was weak. I gave in."

"Are you saying you were unfaithful?"

"Yes," Dante said.

The priest sat in silence for a while and Dante became anxious. "What should I do?" he asked.

"Do you believe you have a contrite heart?"

"I'm here, aren't I?"

The priest cleared his throat again.

"A sin against your wife is a sin against God."

"I know."

"I will ask you again then, do you believe you have a contrite heart?"

Dante could feel his hot, angered blood move around his body. What does it mean to have a contrite heart, he wanted to ask the priest. "I was trying to do the right thing," he said. He got up. "But now I think this was a mistake."

"Sit down," said the priest.

Dante grabbed the doorknob to the confessional.

"I'm sorry," the priest said. "*Please* sit down." The priest's voice was gentler now. "If you must go, you are free to go. I won't hold you here. But I would like you to stay and continue."

Dante sat back down. He grappled with what to do, what to say. The priest was silent and patient. Finally, Dante said. "I fight with my son. Sometimes I want to sock him in the face."

"Have you ever hurt your son?"

"I never hit him."

"Why do you want to sock him in the face?"

"He belittles me. Tries to analyze me. It's disrespectful."

"Do you love your son?"

"Of course I love my son. I wanted him to be a man and do the right thing. I had to make sure he was on the right path."

"And you know for sure what path he should take?"

"I have a good idea, yes."

"Do you ever ask him what he thinks he should do? Do you ask him things? Do you ask him how he is?"

"I know how he is. It's obvious. He's confused."

"Perhaps you should consider pride," the priest said, firmly.

The word was one he did not expect and seemed foreign, like it was from another language.

"I want you to do something nice for your wife," the priest said. "Something that will make her happy. Something substantial and requires effort on your part. And I want you to pray for humility. Pray for you and pray for me."

Dante left the church and walked past his house. He walked past the train station, past the cemetery and the liquor store, past the dump and the animal shelter. Slowly, his hot blood began to cool down. He noticed the simple things while he walked, the gravel on the road, the way the grass pushes through the cracks on the sidewalk, the dead things, dented cans, silt and broken glass, people meandering in their yards, the way sheets of a newspaper are carried by a gust of wind, all the banal things of the world, all the tossed away items. He eventually settled into retirement and learned to play golf and relax. He took Florence to Italy to see the Sistine Chapel and then to Jerusalem, and went walking on Sundays, a pilgrimage to the beach about five miles from his house. It calmed him and eased his anxiety.

Walking, Dante thought, was one of the humblest things you can do.

A door opened in the dark and light poured in from the hallway. His son Bartholomew called to him. There was worry in his voice. Dante saw his son coming into the dark room with a wonderful light behind him. He told him to turn on the light in the room. Florence came in, set up a folding table, went out and returned with a bowl of water and shaving cream. She left them alone, shut the door.

Bardo pulled up a chair and sat down next to his father. He sprayed the shaving cream in his hands and lathered up his father's face. When his son's hands touched his face, Dante felt how gentle they were, tentative. It made him sad.

Immediately his son misunderstood him. "Why are you looking at me like that?" Bardo asked. "Don't you trust me?"

"Of course I trust you. Don't be silly. It's just that every time you shave, you have a bloodied piece of tissue stuck to your cheek. I just want you to take it easy. That razor is sharp."

"This is a good exercise, Dad. Let's see how we do."

"Does *everything* have to be about our relationship?"

Bardo looked at Dante as he maneuvered the razor about his chin; he looked back and forth at Dante's expression and checked the path of the razor, making sure it was evenly clearing the foam. He shook the razor in the water, dipped it in to wash it off.

"No Dad, not everything has to do with our relationship. But this does. Lift your chin."

Dante tilted his head, looked at Bardo out of the corner of his eye. He said, "I think it was fine."

"What?"

"The relationship. It was good enough."

"You don't think we could have been closer?"

"I think we were close enough."

Bardo flicked the razor again, looked at his father, turned to do the other side of his face. Dante watched his son's expression; he looked hurt.

"What, you don't think so?"

"Dad, stay still. You keep leaning back."

"How close did you wanna be?"

Bardo dunked the razor in the tub of water, the hairs spread into the water like fleas.

"You remember that night when I was down at PJ's, hanging out in the parking lot with some friends?"

Dante's mind illuminated with memory how the headlights of his Grand Prix found his son's white pants as he sprinted through the parking lot, his friends scattering.

"I wanted you to get in the car. You were going off into the alley, into the darkness. You weren't watching where you were going," Dante said.

"You chased me like I was a criminal. This was how I always felt—like I was guilty of something."

"You were arrested for smoking pot with those hippies. And you went back to the very same place. You were lucky I got there before the cops did."

"That's not the point. The point is how I felt. How I always felt. How you've made me feel. I wish it was different. I hoped it would be. But now it's only going to ever be what it was."

Bardo placed the razor on the folding table, then he stopped and looked at his father.

"There you are, perfectly clean shaven. Not one nick."

Dante reached up his hand to feel his face. It felt smooth.

"Huh. You did a good job."

His son looked at him, into his eyes. "Dad . . ." he said.

Dante saw his son's face change from that of a man's to the boy he once was, framed by the mirror behind him. Tears welled in his son's eyes. He reached out to grab his Bardo's wrist. "No, don't" he said. "It's okay. We may not have seen eye-to-eye on a lot of things, but that's okay. I want you to know it, before it's too late. It's all okay with me. Everything."

Bardo looked away, toward the window.

"It's okay. Don't cry. Everything is going to be alright."

Bardo bowed his head and wept.

The mirror became a window, through which he could see his daughter, sitting at the table, smoking, thinking, just like he used to before he quit twenty years ago. They left her in a room full of boxes and a serving of chow mein in the refrigerator. He tried to give her a wad of cash from his pocket but she wouldn't accept it, so he stuffed it between the bare mattress and box spring set up in the bedroom. He would tell her about it later, after she had gathered herself.

He and Florence drove home afterward. "That son of a bitch," Florence said.

Dante accompanied his wife inside their house, poured himself a beer and went to sit on the porch to look at the sky. The sky had a way of easing Dante's nerves; he made it part of his routine to watch how the twilight sky moved its clouds over the church, how the clouds seemed to reach for one another, delicate arms of vapor stretching, touching. But tonight, it was dark and the clouds were bunched up, covering the stars. Dante finished his beer and went back to his car. He started the engine and backed out of the driveway and went back to Nicoletta's apartment, shut the car off and sat there for a while, wondering what he should do. At some point in his life, he was going to have to practice faith, like Florence, and let it all go.

"Faith," the devil scoffed. "You have only vague ideas. That isn't good enough."

He left the car and climbed the stairs to his daughter's apartment. From the landing, he could see into her window; it was bare and exposed the insides of the lighted apartment like skin pulled away to uncover a bone, something you weren't supposed to see. He saw her there, a cigarette in her hand, her face was solemn, her eyes staring at something on the floor. He thought of Meryl. Anger rose in his heart; he would not have his daughter become the same woman. He waited. Somewhere in the distance lightning flashed, thunder rumbled. He waited for her to give him a sign to go to her. She stubbed out her cigarette, placed her hands on her legs and thought for a moment, staring at the blankness of the table, before she rose. Then she got up in one motion and left the room. He had recognized himself then, in this pensive action, in the way she placed her hands on the tops of her thighs and the way she rose, with conviction. He descended the stairs, put the keys back in the ignition, started the car, and drove back home.

The church across the street was silent; there were no bells at night to call the hours. The bedroom door was not completely closed and let in some light that hit the mirror and was scattered in the mists. Dante watched as the light and the mists took on a form. He reached for his spectacles on the night table and put them on. In the glass was something he had never seen before: it was a creature with its wings folded. And then, slowly, the wings unfurled, feather by feather, until he could see the full wingspan of the angel in the mirror. It had the face of a woman looking down at something, and when she raised her head, he saw that the face was that of his daughter, Carmen.

"What are you going to do, follow her again on her date? Leave her alone. Let her have some fun," Florence said.

"I know how a young man thinks."

He grabbed his hat and coat, put his hand on the door and then heard the frantic steps up the front stairs. The storm door swung open and the knob twisted in his hands.

She opened the door and gasped. Then she slid past him, went to the closet, stuffed her coat in, leapt up the stairs two at a time and turned around. It was a face he had seen every day of his life for so many years, it was a face beaming through the mist—glorious.

"Good night, Daddy," she said.

Dante wailed with grief at the thought of leaving them. The sound of agony filled the house and settled into the bodies of his loved ones. They feared him now more than they ever had, because his suffering far surpassed their own, and because they knew they would lose him. Shamefully, they scattered to other rooms, hid, blocked the sound of his cries from their ears. But in the glory of the early morning, he saw that someone placed roses on the dresser in front of the mirror. The sweet smell of the roses, white, pure, engulfing, the sweet smell of life filled the room. Dante stopped his wailing, bowed his head, and died.

CHAPTER 2
THE DEVOTED
NICOLETTA

The first time I met Sabine, it was in a dream. I had seen her before, at the supermarket, at the bank, always with her daughter, a girl of about eleven with dark hair and light emerald eyes like her mother. In my mind, I referred to her as "the woman"; the woman with bronze hands and a red scarf, the mulatto woman, displaced in this Long Island town, an anomaly. In Bohack's, she chose her oranges scrupulously, smelled the freshly baked bread in its paper bag, ordered her meat with precision, "Cut the ham a quarter of an inch thick, please." In the bank, the tellers referred to her as Ms. Toulouise, yes, Ms. Toulouise, here's your deposit slip, Ms. Toulouise, anything else, Ms. Toulouise, and she walked past the rest of us in line with her head high and a determined stride, her daughter in tow, as if they always had a destination. I watched her and wondered what her life had been like to manifest in her such confidence.

In the dream, she was in a room in a house on Northport Harbor, where my father used to take my son to look at the boats. It was an old house—my grandmother's, although hers was technically in Westbury—and in the living room Sabine was arranging white roses in a vase when I walked in. No one else was with her in the kitchen or in the living room, or upstairs, where my sister and I slept sometimes when my mother left my father after a fight and we spent the weekend in Westbury. But there were people, sleeping, talking, eating, some nameless, some named, crowded in the musty light of the basement: my grandmother in her housedress watching *I Love Lucy*, my uncle Tony—a man who used to fold dollars into my palms during family gatherings. These people were all known to be dead, but in the dream, there was some mistake, or maybe it was that the living had gotten it wrong—how they perceived death—that it really wasn't an end. And that was it. There was no real event, nothing happened, I just showed up in the house with Sabine arranging roses and the dead people mulling around in the basement.

I didn't pay the dream any mind at first. My brother Bardo, who studied Freud, said that dreams were repressed desires, and I assumed that this was exactly what it was. My father was not yet dead from the cancer, and in a locked room in my mind, I believed that he had the choice to rule against death and return at will, as the people in the dream had. He would not return Christlike in a white robe of glory, but as himself, as if he temporarily went somewhere else for a few weeks, and then took up where he left off.

It was Saturday and it was February, but the sun was shining, so I dressed Thomas and took him to the harbor to the playground, where my father used to go with him. I needed to get out, to not let my thoughts fester into anxiety or feeling sorry for myself. I am always battling this need.

I dressed Thomas in his jacket and boots, hat, scarf, and mittens, and in doing this I remembered that wretched woman's face—the woman who reprimanded me last year for not taking care of my son. That day I had only dressed Thomas in his parka, thinking the day would be warmer than it was, and the gray clouds soon squelched the sun, and it quickly turned bitter cold. She made a beeline straight for us, was one of those women who scope out strollers and carriages, because children were her specialty. After making goo-goo faces, she chastised me: "His hands are red and cold! He needs his mittens! Where are his mittens! And his hat! Do you know that the body loses most of its heat through the head?" I apologized profusely, made an excuse about the weather and then scooped up my son and quickly extracted him from the scene, as the cold damp wind off the harbor blew even harder. I placed him in the car, and rubbing his hands with mine, blew my warm breath into his hands. I felt like a criminal who had been caught: she had found me out, how inept I was at being a mother.

My Buick started on the third try. "Come on car, come on, one more time, just give me one more time. Tomorrow it will be warmer, Let's go!" Thomas let out a little laugh. *Huh huh*, he said. He likes it when I talk to the car. I fumbled with the heater and the radio at the same time and the chill of winter and the smell of engine parts came wafting out of the vent. "Fine," I said, lowering the blower and backing out of the parking space quickly, crushing my garbage can lid. I shouldn't have had the coffee. I know that coffee makes my anxiety worse, and I still drink it, because it's there, and it's morning, and I like the aroma that says *morning* when it percolates, and the feeling of hope and renewal that a day could bring. Because my mother always drank coffee and she used to tell us when we wanted something from her, "Not till I have had my coffee," so I equate it with morning, mothering, and this is what I desire most of all, to be normal, and not feel like I am about to plunge into an abyss.

As we were driving, I thought of my father dying in his bed and how later we would visit him, because it made him happy to see Thomas, and how he would tell his grandson that when he is well and out of the bed, they would go to the park and see the boats. And I thought to myself, is he right? How will he get out from under the mound of aberrant flesh? I looked at Thomas in the back seat. "Thomas, honey, Mommy is especially crazy today," and he smiled, giving me a look that tells me today is absolutely no different from any other day. I took a few big breaths and stepped on the gas, fumbling again with the heat and the radio and chastising myself in my head with the voice of the woman: "Concentrate on the road! Do you know how many accidents have been had by fumbling with the heater and the radio at the same time?"

It was cold at the park and there was no one else there. The snow had melted and froze into ice around the swings and slide, and Thomas was padded enough, but with my luck, I would fall and break my ass. So, we went to a neighborhood café and sat in a room with warm bodies that fogged up the windows, and I had a bagel and Thomas a donut. Soon the greasy hash browns and runny eggs disgusted me; the fogged-up windows from the heat of bodies and their proximity heightened my anxiety—I had to leave. I asked the waitress for the check and scrambled for bills in my purse: this is how it was when I was in public. It always seemed like a good idea to get out, but then when I was out, amidst other people, I began to retreat inside myself. No, retreat is not the word—the word is drown—drown inside myself, occupied with errant thoughts of not being able to escape, of not being able to breathe, of not being able to speak, of panicking uncontrollably, of being out of control and everyone around me seeing it. It wasn't normal, the continuous hot rushes of panic: something was out of balance, but I had no idea how to fix it. I confided in Bardo; he was the one who gave me the term for it: angst. He said it was an age-old human condition, but I felt like I was the only one feeling it.

For the most part, I am good at faking normalcy. I doubt for a second that waitress, or anyone else in that café, for that matter, suspected I was having a panic attack. They were all living their lives, talking, laughing, being light-hearted on a Saturday morning in a café in a sleepy coastal town. If everyone around me was fooled by my performance of normalcy, my son was especially fooled and submits to the plan every step of the way on a regular basis. I am thankful for that.

I had noticed that a flower shop opened up next door, and I thought of the dream and the roses. It would be good to bring roses to my father, to brighten up his room. He was not a man who would buy flowers, not even for my mother. He bought her jewelry instead, because it had longevity, and for sure he would not want me to "waste my money" but in the backyard, he cultivated a white rose bush to grow over an arbor and it was his pride and joy. "See how it's filled out, nice?" he'd say every June. So, I decided to buy him roses, to remind him of the beauty of that vivacious hedge, to take his mind off his suffering and to give myself a meaningful task.

We walked into the florist shop and I immediately felt better. It was quiet except for the trickling of water somewhere. Plants filled the room, flowers in baskets, elegant stone statues with somber faces, soft moss covering cement urns and red and pink Valentine bouquets; it was lush and serene and all the angst I had felt only moments before drained away. A girl came from the back room. I recognized her immediately. She had a sketchbook and colored pencils and sat down at the counter. "Maman!" She called to the open door behind her. "There is a lady here!" I immediately picked up Thomas, afraid he would destroy one of the slender statues.

It was Mrs. Toulouise who came from the back room carrying yellow tulips in a glass vase. She placed the tulips on the countertop and the daughter immediately started to draw them. I remembered the dream then, how she was the one arranging the roses, and it seemed uncanny then, that I had happened upon the flower shop and the woman in it was the same woman I dreamt about. Mrs. Toulouise's hair was done up neatly in braids; she had full lips and green eyes, the kind of eyes that seemed unworldly. Her skin—flawless. She wore a cashmere sweater and a delicate freshwater pearl necklace, had the appearance of being born in a faraway exotic place; it only seemed logical that she surrounded herself with floral beauty. This was something some people knew how to do: buffer themselves from the world with beautiful things. I had neither the time nor the money for beautiful things. I was embarrassed by my woolen hat that fit too low on my brow because I had worn and washed it year after year. My coat was given to me by my sister Carmen and despite the warmth it afforded me, the scent of it was Carmen's scent, and always reminded me that I settle for hand-me-downs and practicality, and demanded virtually nothing from life.

"Would the boy like a cookie?" Mrs. Toulouise asked. Her voice was soft and musical.

"We made heart-shaped cookies for Valentine's Day," the girl said.

"Would you like a cookie?" I asked Thomas, and he buried his face in my coat, shyly.

"Sure," I said.

Mrs. Toulouise brought out a dish of pink and red hearts, each outlined formally with delicate white icing. We all took a cookie and while we were eating them, Mrs. Toulouise looked at me more intently. "Do I know you?" she asked.

"We've seen each other around town, I'm sure," I said. "I am Nicky."

"Sabine," she said, and extended her hand. I took note of her finely manicured nails.

"I'd like to buy a half-dozen white roses," I said.

"Ah yes, we have those over here."

There was a sliding glass door and behind it buckets of flowers. Sabine picked out six long-stemmed white roses and arranged them with evergreen in tissue paper and tied it with a satin bow. I set Thomas down and he grabbed my leg as he ate the rest of his cookie, dropping crumbs on the ceramic tiled floor. I noticed then, a small sign next to the door to the backroom. It read "Clairvoyant."

"Who is the clairvoyant?" I asked.

"I am," Sabine said.

"You are a psychic?"

"If you want to call it that."

"What would you call it?"

"I call it 'having a gift.'"

"Do you interpret dreams?"

"Of course."

She rang up the roses in the cash register, and I unzipped my purse and reached for my wallet. There was the water trickling, yes, I noticed that, but also, a new feeling. It was a new internal reference point—one of intrigue.

"These roses are for my father. He is dying. I had a dream you were arranging these flowers in a vase and there were dead people around you."

"So, you have the gift too," Sabine said.

"Ordinarily I am not receptive to anything but my own suffering."

"That's how it is for everyone."

"I find that hard to believe."

Sabine smiled. "Maybe something is shifting."

"Why would I need to bring him roses? What does it mean?"

"The roses themselves mean nothing. It's you giving them to him that matters. It is an act of love. It's necessary that the dying know we love them. It fortifies them for the transition."

Thomas tugged at my leg. "Cookie," he said, looking down at half his cookie on the floor.

"Oh honey," I said, and he whimpered.

"Here, take some more for later," Sabine said, wrapping up two more cookies in tissue paper. And here is my card, if you need to talk."

The card was handwritten in calligraphy. *Sabine Toulouise, Clairvoyant.* She gave me a carry-all bag for the roses and cookies, as she was handing it to me, she stopped a moment and I saw the flash across her eyes.

"Has he come into your life yet?" she asked.

"I'm sorry?"

"The devoted. Has he come to you yet?"

A group of people came in at that moment—last minute Valentine shoppers; one of them approached Sabine with an arrangement in a vase, "Excuse me, how much for the bouquet?" Sabine surreptitiously placed her card in my bag and went to wait on the man, while I took the bag in one arm and Thomas in the other, and ducked out of the store.

The night my father died, my sister and I sat in the dark in the living room listening to his wailing. We had taken turns caring for him for several days, and then he stopped talking, eating, and drinking and slipped into a deep sleep. My mother had one of the older priests from the rectory across the street give him his last rites. Afterward, we applied warm cloths to his brow and cool cloths for his parched lips and shifted his arms and legs to assuage the pain of bed sores. A day later and he became visibly restless and started to wail; his tortured cries filled the house. They paralyzed us; unlike my mother who had left us to pray the rosary at church, Carmen and I stayed to listen to it, as if it were our penance. Then he stopped just before midnight. We went in and saw that his mouth had sprung open like a trap door; his face was distorted because the life had gone out of him. I put the sheet over him; we could not look at his face. On the dresser, the roses seemed impotent; some were wilted and losing their petals, and I felt ridiculous for bringing them, thinking what a fool I was to believe my actions truly had meaning. Because at that point when my father died, nothing had meaning. Carmen called the funeral parlor and they came for him. We could not watch them take the body out of the house, so we went to bed and tried to sleep.

The next morning the light poured in gloriously through the thinly veiled windows. Carmen was huddled up against the wall, asleep, so I closed the shades, put on my shoes, grabbed my coat, and went out, still dressed from last night. Outside, there was birdsong and the air had a new warmth to it. I went to my car and saw a dove perched on the driver sideview mirror. It seemed as if it had fallen asleep in the sunlight and just when I noticed it, sprung up and flew away.

My ex-husband Al wasn't really a man when I married him, and I wasn't really a woman. He was a proto-man and I was a proto-woman; we were partially formed people who had vague ideas of what they wanted for themselves. I assumed Al would be like Richard, my sister's husband, who wooed her, married her, provided for her. And he assumed I would want sex every night, like he did. Given two prominent examples in my father and Richard, I never really doubted that Al would be a decent husband and provider, because according to my mother, "this is what men do." And in the general scheme of things, Al played the part well; he did buy us a house (with his stepfather's money). He did have a steady job as a carpenter, although to pay the mortgage, I had to work as well—something Carmen never had to do. Periodically, Al had to take work in upstate New York, when work around here was scarce, and would, at times, be gone for weeks at a time. I had no hint of any deviation in his devotion to me until my brother called to tell me he saw Al having breakfast with a woman at Fred's Diner.

"She was probably just a client," I said.

"What client sits on the same side of the table and puts her tongue in his ear?" he asked.

We were in the throes of divorce when I found out I was pregnant. When I told my parents, my mother was confused and my father just sat there and didn't say a word. "We will help you, Nicky," my sister Carmen said, who at this point had a three-year-old and another on the way, herself.

"How are you supposed to be mother and father to this baby?" my mother asked.

"We will help you," Carmen said again. She looked at my mother. "Right, Ma? She needs help, so we will help her."

My mother shook her head. I was an embarrassment to her.

My father sat there in silence, staring at the marble tile on the kitchen floor, making me unbearably anxious.

"Dad. Daddy, say something," said Carmen.

"I'll take it!" I yelled, in a shrill, out-of-control voice. I turned around to face my father, took a deep breath. "Did you hear me? I said I'll take it. Just the baby. Never mind the husband. I'll take the baby. Just the baby is fine with me!"

"What do you mean just the baby is fine with you. It's not fine. It takes a lot to raise a kid. Stop being naïve," my father said. "You're always doing things the hard way," he said. "You always make more work for yourself. You should have never married that bum in the first place."

"It's not doing things the hard way. It's taking what comes. What's given to me."

"That's not how I raised you," my mother said. "Take what's given to you. *Jeezis.*"

"Easy for you to say, you already have a husband," I murmured.

Carmen chimed in, "We're not going to get anywhere playing the blame game. Nicky is going to have a baby and we're going to embrace this baby and help her give him a fine life. This is what we're going to do."

And eventually they did. No questions asked.

It was September when I asked my mother to babysit on Sunday afternoons so I could go and walk the beach alone. Walking the beach was a way for me to mimic my father and be close to him. Bardo said my father's Sunday pilgrimages to the Long Island Sound were a sign of self-actualization. He had reached a place in his life where he was no longer frustrated or yearning for something; he had reached the point where he could enjoy his own company and appreciate everything around him. "It's the highest state of mind anyone could achieve," my brother said.

The beach in September is a forgotten place. Only a few people mingle here now; the throngs of bathers are off doing other more pressing things. What impresses me is the clarity of the air, how the landscape is a landscape without hindrance; how everything is immediately available to me in its purest state; the sea is remarkably blue, lapping in small waves that swish up the sand; the sand is cool and molds easily to the shapes of my feet. The few people present are here to grasp on to something fleeting, the last of the summer sun against their skin, the last swim of the season. I watch the sea make its deposits: driftwood, broken buoy parts, shells. When I head toward the parking lot and the sand has muffled the sounds of the gulls, I feel calm, noticeably different from how I arrived. But there is also a sadness, a yearning inside me for something I cannot name.

One Sunday, something strange happened. It was colder, and a queer fog rolled in from the water; I lost my sense of direction. The dunes were there and then they weren't; the sea dissolved into the sky in a haze of white. It was so quick—the way everything was swallowed up—and I started to feel that familiar rise of panic. Then I looked down and there were petals strewn in the sand, as if someone had picked apart a white rose and let the petals fall where they may. I followed them thinking of the roses I placed at my father's deathbed. Was he leading me out of the fog? The feeling of him helping me brought tears to my eyes, and I bent down to retrieve the petals in the sand—moist, cool, delicate things. I followed them to a path through the brush where I could see the parking lot. The pounding in my heart slowed, and I had that wash of relief that the panic was over and I was safe. But then, when I was shuffling in my purse for my keys to open my car door, I noticed a man opening his own car door a few parking spaces away. I made note of his rolled-up jeans. The mists and wind drifted past him and just as he opened the door and got in, the wind picked up something from his pocket and blew it toward me. I went to fetch it, but by the time I retrieved it, the car was already driving away. I unfolded the note and read the words written on the page: *Forgive me.*

That night, I dreamt of a woman dancing. The dancer wore a long white tutu and had dark hair like me, and dark eyes. Then, almost as if she had wings, she leapt through the air and went out the window.

The next week when I went to the beach, I saw the man again, in the same rolled up jeans. This time he was sitting on a bench cleaning his feet. He washed them slowly and carefully with the water from the faucet that extended from the boardwalk. Then he patted them dry with a small towel. He was traditionally handsome, almost as if he were the model for the Ken doll, tall, square shoulders, fine cheekbones, a square jaw. Visions of things manifested inside me: a closet of clothes, a dining room table with lit candles, a car door opening, a woman in a wedding gown in front of a full-length mirror. Ballet shoes hanging in a closet. A lake with a dock. Bicycles. *Vines,* I said aloud. *They're rooting inside me like vines.*

I was distracted by the visions and almost paralyzed by them, they had such weight. He put on his second sandal, having wiped his second foot, and was now making ready to go. I casually walked forward and sat down at the end of the bench. The sea was a majestic blue in the background and a family was cooking sausages on a hibachi just beyond the boardwalk. I thought of my own family then, how we too used to gather here.

"What a fine night for a cookout," he said to me, expecting to make casual conversation with a stranger. My heart beat wildly against my ribs and my face began to flush. I wanted to flee.

"Yes," I said.

"The beach is kinder in September; do you agree?" he said, fixing the heel of his sandal. And then he looked up, and I saw his eyes and as I looked into them, I saw they were multi-faceted, as a gem might be multi-faceted when light strikes it. He hesitated then, and his countenance changed from one engaging in casual conversation with a stranger to one that was visibly struck with apprehension. He became quiet, looked down at the planks of the boardwalk. The wind rustled his soft, loose cotton shirt; he cleared his throat. "I'm sorry," he said. "You have an uncanny resemblance to someone I used to know."

"Oh," I said, laughing awkwardly. "Well, that is something I don't hear every day."

He continued to look at me, my face, my hands, the T-shirt that said "Virginia is for Lovers," a relic from my trip to Virginia Beach with Al, my cut-off shorts and flip flops. I wondered what he thought of my nose; surely this other woman's nose wasn't as big as mine, an Italian-style honker that always made me feel ugly and insecure. I was just a local girl, a commoner, nothing, I was certain, like the woman he associated himself with. But the breeze was cool and calm and perfectly satisfying on my skin. And upon a second look, I noticed that this man was staring at me, perplexed, and I felt somewhat comforted that he was struggling with something too.

"But—. It is—." He shook his head. "I am sorry."

I thought then, of the note.

"Do you live around here?" he asked.

"All my life."

"I was born and raised in New Jersey, but I moved here from the Midwest. Chicago."

"I've never been there," I said. "Never been to a lot of places."

"A provincial girl, then."

I smiled and nodded politely, making a note to look up the word "provincial." "What brought you here?" I asked.

"A transfer. For… work."

The vines began to grow again, and bloom; the woman standing in front of the mirror in white was the most prominent. She was wearing a simple pearl necklace, I saw that clearly, and, yes, a veil, but there was something significant about the veil.

"The veil." I said, "there is something significant about the veil. The lace of the veil was intricate and from a faraway place. The lace itself had a history."

"I'm sorry?"

"The other woman was a bride, wasn't she. And a dancer. A ballet dancer. I dreamt of her." His brow wrinkled as he tried to process what I said. I tried to process what I said, because I said it without thinking, without knowing exactly what I was talking about.

"Are you a medium?"

"No," I said. "I mean, maybe. I don't know. This is all new to me."

"Almost a bride," he said. "She was almost a bride. And yes, she was a ballet dancer."

"Oh." I looked down at the seasoned wood, precarious in places, with regard to splinters.

"It was years ago," he said, watching the family sitting and eating, tossing a football, gossiping. "We were never married, because she passed away. But you said you dreamt of her? Tell me, what else do you know?"

I looked into his face, his multi-faceted eyes. "That she is close," I said.

The crying of the gulls in mid-air made the place seem mournful. There was a couple walking along the beach, the woman had a scarf that rippled in the wind in a romantic fashion and the man wore a gentleman's hat, like the kind people wear at summer tennis events. I could not deny the feeling that I had, sitting there with the man. I felt powerful. Confident.

"She is close," he reiterated. "The lace veil was her grandmother's. It was made in Venice by a family merchant, and it traveled the Atlantic Ocean when her family emigrated. A family heirloom. She was very excited to wear it."

"It must've been beautiful. She must've been beautiful."

"It was. She—was." I looked at the place where his hair met his neck, just behind his ear. It was an intimate place that she must've known. "Who are you?" he asked. "I mean, what is your name?"

I told him my name. He told me his name: Robert Kirton. He said he had an appointment, that he had to go, but he took my number and wanted to meet up again. I told him I wasn't sure I would have any more information. This wasn't something I did on a regular basis. "Maybe it's this place," I said. "Maybe it's the beach. The serenity here. The simplicity." He agreed. "Maybe there is nothing more I have to say," I said. He nodded his head in agreement and walked to his car.

My first hint of the world of fate happened after I graduated high school. I was sitting with my friend Lucia in her room and we were talking about her parents' relationship. Lucia's family had money; her father was a builder who built homes for the rich in the Hamptons. Whenever I visited her in her home, her parents were off doing important things and the only one roaming about was her grandmother, always dressed in black and muttering to herself in Italian. Lucia's house looked like something out of old-world Italy with its marble floors, stucco walls, lions at the end of the driveway. She lived on a hill overlooking Northport Harbor where trees were cleared to make room for rows of grapevines. Being in that house was like being in a mausoleum, with the cool dry air of some mystery accompanying the silence. We had picnics among the grapes and talked about boys and ate the grapes— in one sweet taste I sensed a land far away and history of a people to whom I was linked by blood but barely understood. Lucia's family had decided she should go to nursing school and possibly become a doctor. Her Italian relatives were peasants, like mine, but her father's success had reshaped the family's ideas of how life should go and this trickled down to Lucia, who had no interest in nursing whatsoever. Like her father, Lucia's mother had done well for herself; when she arrived in America at nineteen, she worked as a seamstress in the sweatshops in Manhattan, like my grandmother had, but was now a designer of women's clothes. Lucia had no interest in designing clothes; her only interest was in boys and sneaking out in the middle of the night to go driving in cars with them.

On this particular evening with Lucia on her bed with a painting of Tuscany above us and a cat purring in her lap, that I learned her family had a secret. It was obvious there was love lost between her parents: at dinner one noticed they hardly looked at one another. Her mother coolly smoked after the meal, asked me superficial questions, and her father hid behind the evening paper. Her grandmother chattered in Italian and her mother would give her one-word answers. It was awkward, and I hated to eat dinner with them, but Lucia insisted, because she was an only child and felt lonesome most of the time.

That day, Lucia broached the issue. "Don't think I am unaware of the strangeness of my parent's marriage. They hate one another. I wish they would just divorce, but they won't, because of my grandmother and the Church."

"Why do they hate each other?"

"Because something happened. Something changed around the time I was five. It wasn't always like this. They used to laugh and go out to dinner and to parties and dancing. They had friends over for drinks and swimming in the pool. But that all stopped. The doors of our house are now closed to outsiders. Now all they do is work. I think my father resents my mother for her job. I think he wants her home. But here in America, she considers herself a liberated woman."

Lying in Lucia's bed that night as she slept next to me with soft rollers in her hair secured by one of her grandmother's black lace kerchiefs, I heard a voice inside me that said I would know their secret like I know the sound of my own name.

While Lucia went on to nursing school, I floundered about, unsure of what to do with my life. I put in an application to start medical secretary school, but this wouldn't be until next year, because I had missed the year's deadline. I mostly lay about getting fat and watching television sitcoms, miserable and hopeless. It was then that my mother got a call from Lucia's father. He needed someone to perform various jobs for him at his construction company: some secretarial (I had learned how to type and write shorthand in high school) and also clean the newly constructed homes he was building in the Hamptons. I leapt at the chance.

The next day, I took the train to Kings Park where he had his office. The walkway to the office had fine stonework, like the grounds of the house in Northport. There was a black marble tile that read "Neapolitan Brothers Construction" in gold and a receptionist with fashionable red hair and pink lipstick smoking at a desk. She had fine arched eyebrows, like Sophia Loren and had an Italian accent, and looked me over from head to toe, as if she suspected I was up to something, surmising what a girl like me could possibly want with a construction company. I told her I was here to meet with Mr. Ricci, and she yelled for Gregorio over her shoulder and then he appeared, Lucia's father, standing in a doorway, and I felt like I was looking at him for the first time.

I knew what I was getting myself into, and I was perfectly willing, because I was flattered to have a man like Gregorio, a powerful man, a handsome man with striking blue eyes, olive skin, and salt and pepper hair, pay attention to me. I had always been afraid of him, because he was so quiet and imposing, and he had this way about him that you could tell he was disgruntled by life, and a private person—he didn't want to be bothered with anyone. I had no idea he was interested in me from my interactions at his house. That first day Gregorio Ricci drove me in his fancy convertible to the Hamptons, to a mansion with turrets and open windows high above the sea grass. There was a long wooden staircase to the beach and a swimming pool and a cabana. The newly built house was empty, all glass and stone and echoes of the carpenters yelling in Italian dialect, banging nails into wood, sawing. Gregorio was a different man then; he wasn't the silent and imposing figure that watched over the Ricci compound high in the hills overlooking Northport Harbor, he was kind, and insightful, and profound, and interesting. This job of washing newly tiled floors, bathrooms, and windows above the dunes was a cover up for a relationship he wanted to have with me. It almost felt right that he should put his hand on my knee, driving his expensive car around the curves of eastern Long Island. We'd go to roadside cafes and eat soft crab sandwiches and he'd tell me the stories of his family, how his father built a masonry business in Naples only to drown in a quarry because he never learned to swim. And we talked about death, because he thought about it a lot, because his mother was a witch who communicated with the dead and had spells and potions for all kinds of situations and illnesses as well as a propensity for interpreting dreams. "There's something about you," he told me on one of those first forays out for lunch. "You are like her—my mother, the *strega*."

He always told me he had more money than he knew what to do with. It had always been easy for him to make money. But money wasn't everything. He learned this when he had a mild heart attack a few years ago, while he was in Italy for the summer, and it changed his life. "I wanted you to come and work for me, because I knew you were lost," he told me. "And I thought I could help you."

I wasn't really sure what great realization he had had after the heart attack. It was all sort of vague. He insisted that he had learned to appreciate the little things, the taste of a good glass of wine. A swim in the sea in the morning. He showed me a postcard he kept in the glove compartment of his car. It was of stars in space with an arrow pointing to a spec. "You are here," it said. "We must not forget how insignificant we really are in the grand scheme of things." He came to fetch me every day, after I had swept and mopped the floors and cleaned the toilets, newly positioned in the bathrooms. He brought me out to lunch, or to eat sandwiches on the beach, and I followed him out of the house feeling this vibration of excitement in my body, making note of the workers who muttered under their breath in Italian.

He took my hand and we walked along the beach and told me that I need not worry because we would just hold hands. We were friends who held hands, like they did in Italy. And then once we had a picnic in the dunes and he kissed me and I tasted the onions from his tuna sandwich in his mouth. I was repulsed, but when he said, "Again," I kissed him again, because to not kiss him might anger him or cause me to fall out of favor and for such an insignificant being, I needed to have all the favor I could get. So, we only kissed and I believed that would be it, and I did not think of Lucia or her mother at all, because that would mean tarnishing the euphoria I felt by being lavished.

Gregorio did not regale me with jewels; he did not take me to fancy restaurants. He gave me stones, cobblestones that he engraved words into like "persevere," and "hope," and "fortitude." These stones were small, about the size of my palm, and I was fond of holding one or the other, depending on what word I felt like carrying around. They were smooth, old. "What time has done to these," he said, referring to the rocks, "it will do to us."

But I refused to think about what was really on his mind, about my body pressed against his body, a young woman's naked body pressed against the body of an older man, because it was then that I became acutely aware that he was a father, like my own father. My friend's father. It seemed taboo and wrong, and I was not desperate enough to break through that mental obstruction. I reconciled with the fact that I had to start pushing him away when he put his hand on my breast or started to caress my thighs. He started talking about what it would be like if we became intimate, where it could happen. I had to distract him. "There's something wrong," I said. "There's something wrong between you and your wife. You are cold with one another. Your marriage is dead. Why?"

And something shifted then. I had brought him down to Earth, grounded him by dispelling the fantasy. "She slept with my brother. When I was away in Italy. They slept together. It was a mistake: a one-time event, but that one-time event had made a child. This is the way the math worked out, you know what I mean? I was not there. She had an abortion. She aborted it and now I hate her for two reasons: one that she cheated on me, and the other that she was *that* kind of woman."

And there it was: the big secret. Life had arranged itself in a way that I would never have anticipated that night Lucia told me of her parents' secret. I became displaced, out of my traditional role of "child" and into the higher role of lover and confidant so that this information would be passed on to me. But I had no idea why. It made no real sense why I had to know this. There was nothing dire I needed to do with this information; there was no moral or ethical task to complete. I didn't feel it was necessary to tell Lucia; she was going on with her life, and it would only bring disruption. It was simply a knowing. And once this information had revealed itself, the relationship ended abruptly. And it was I who ended it, but not by choice.

My parents had no clue I was having an affair with a married man, let alone my best friend's father. They were just happy to have me out of the house. Sometimes, after work, I would walk to Memorial Park on the harbor to recollect and bask in the titillating effects of the day. It was here that I saw Lucia's grandmother, dressed in black, walking with her hands clasped behind her back, talking if someone was walking right beside her. I noticed her and ducked. She passed me and walked toward the garden, and I went in the opposite direction toward the gazebo at the end of the wharf. I sat on one of the benches there and remembered how Lucia and I used to come here to wait for the neighborhood boys to take us out in their father's boats to drink out on the harbor. Boys my age didn't really get me; they saw in me something I couldn't see in myself: a need to have someone reconcile the confusion and loneliness inside me, the need for a savior, and they wanted no part of it. I seemed to transcend all that now. I was with someone who wanted to know me, who liked to talk to me, who appreciated my company and what I had to say. This is what I was thinking when someone knocked on the bench in back of me to get my attention. I looked up and Lucia's grandmother loomed above me with a stern expression. "*Puttana!*" She sneered, and she spit on the ground next to my feet. "*Ah Stregatz!*," she said. She then proceeded to curse me out in Italian and passerby gawked at us. "I'm sorry!" I said, and tried walking away from her. She grabbed my arm. "You go home!" she said. "You go home!" And I did, feeling dirty and despicable.

The next day, I called the secretarial school and completed my enrollment to start early. I quit my job with Gregorio. I told him what happened, and he nodded his head, as if he knew. "My mother knows everything. I can get away with nothing. She probably dreamt about us. She knew I was going to have a heart attack because she dreamt that my heart was a crushed apple in my chest."

"She called me a *puttana*, which I know the meaning of, but also a *stregatz*. What is that?"

"Dialect for *strega*. Witch. I told you; my mother knows everything." And that was the last I saw of Gregorio.

Maybe it takes one to know one. Maybe *stregas*, clairvoyants, psychics can sniff each other out. That's why I dreamt about Sabine the way Lucia's grandmother dreamt about me.

My mother refers to the head of the Marion Legion chapter as her "president." We were in the car coming back from food shopping and she was telling me about her and how forgetful she is. Then she tells me that her "president" may have a thing for the new priest at church. "You should see the way her eyes light up when she talks to him. What would a doll like him want with an old lady like her?" she said, chuckling to herself. We pulled onto her street and the priest just so happened to be taking a walk. "Look, there he is! Stop the car!" She rolled down her window. "Father, hello! Getting some exercise?"

The priest waved and then walked toward the car. Immediately I recognized the curve of his jaw.

"Father, this is my daughter Nicoletta. She takes me food shopping, because, you know, I don't have the car anymore and I can't see right."

"Oh yes, the glaucoma," the priest said. He leaned in and I could clearly see his face; there was no doubt that it was him: Robert Kirton, the man I met on the beach.

"Hello," I said, sheepishly.

"Hello," he said with a warm smile. But then it disappeared and he wavered there, peering in through the window, dumbfounded for the second time.

"What a beauteeeful day!" my mother said. "September is such a beauteeeful month; don't you think? It is my favorite."

"Indeed," said Kirton, and then he backed away from the car. "Well, you ladies have yourselves a fine day," he said perfunctorily.

"You too, Father!"

I pulled away from the curb, stealing glances in the rearview to see him stop and turn around. "That's Father Kirton," my mother said. "He's new. Isn't he a doll?"

It was nearly seven months after I first walked into the flower shop that I returned to speak with Sabine. She welcomed me back and we took up the conversation as if only a day had passed. We sat in her back room and drank tea from delicate teacups, dainty and pretty with a painted red rose on each, as Esmerelda, her daughter, drew pictures for Thomas and Thomas tried his hand at drawing his own with Esmerelda gently encouraging him and handing him different colored pencils. It was good to see him interact with someone other than me, someone outside the family. I told Sabine about my predicament, and she, in turn, told me her story.

CHAPTER 3
SABINE'S STORY
HAITI, 1971

My gift started small, knowing where to find misplaced items, or the dates when babies would be born, or if a loved one was sick or in trouble. It became more intense with the visions of my grandmother, who had died ten years before the day she appeared to me in the garden, under the guava tree, looking out at the mountains where the coffee cherries grew. She was not old, as I had known her, but young, just coming of age, the daughter of a renowned plantation owner whose coffee was shipped all over the world. She had long auburn hair and her radiance captivated me, but it came with a price; after seeing her, the migraines would come—first, an aura in the bottom right corner of my vision and then a waving, radiating color that caused a sharp, stabbing pain across my temples and my eyes. The pain lasted for days. My mother called on doctors and apothecaries who gave me pills and elixirs to no avail. When my grandmother's ghost ceased to appear, the rains came, and the mudslides. The machinery rusted; the workers abandoned us for plantations across the border in the Dominican Republic where wages were still petty but guaranteed. My parents sold the plantation house and moved us to a small apartment in the city where we went to school, and my father tried to recuperate his earnings through various business ventures.

My parents had instilled morals and value in my sisters and me; we were the aristocrats, envied by those less fortunate, those whose homes were destroyed by hurricanes. The vagabonds in the streets— those who burned the bones of the dead to live in their tombs—were a constant reminder of the treachery of our country, of how easy it was to fall into ruin. For so long we ate well and mingled with the elite of society, until the elite became the target of *Bébé Doc* and his government and one at a time began to disappear.

My father became quiet and withdrawn. He sold his expensive cars and drank more. He disappeared for hours on end; my mother worried with each absence that he had been abducted or killed by the bands of men running in the streets with machetes. But I knew where he had gone. I had seen it in my dreams, the *vévé* in the shape of a heart—the gate through which the *lwa Erzuli* enters the mortal world. I smelled the rum on his breath, saw him kiss the goddess on the mouth.

The headaches started up again with the recurring dream of the etchings on the floor, delicate filigree made from ash, destroyed by wind, recreated again beneath the feet of the blue veil and the candlelit face of the Virgin Mary—the surrogate for *Erzuli*. Eventually there was a name—Martine; I said it aloud upon waking, confused, because this was the name of my dear aunt, my father's sister.

The headaches had made me weak and short-tempered. One night when my sisters and mother had gone to vespers, and I was alone with my father, my nose started bleeding, and I panicked, thinking that I was being manipulated by the *manbo,* the priestess of *Erzuli.* My father nonchalantly pulled his handkerchief from his pocket, "Why are you getting so excited over a bloody nose?"

I snatched the handkerchief out of his hands. "Why do I dream you kiss your sister on the mouth?"

"*Kisa ou di?*"

"You heard me. There is a name—Martine. Like your sister."

He rummaged for a cigarette in his pocket, tapped it out of the pack and then lit it with nervous hands. "Have you been following me?" he asked.

"No. I told you, I dreamt it. I see the heart-shaped designs of *Erzuli's vévé*. There is a woman—I cannot see her face, but I know her name is Martine."

He looked at me, sizing me up to see if he could confide in me.

"'What is it, Papa?"

"You are not ready," he said. He got up and left before we were done eating. Outside the cacophony of the trucks and motorbikes of the city, the stench of its fumes. I wanted life to go back that way it was; I missed my old room with a door out to the garden and evening birdsong. I missed the way my father used to listen to his jazz records at night and talk quietly with my mother.

The headaches worsened with the summer heat and my mother decided that I should stay for a while with Father Christophe, a family friend, at the seminary in the mountains, for some rest. When we arrived, we sat in his study and she told him all that happened, how she believed I had a gift from God, but that it had "complications," and I needed spiritual guidance.

Father Christophe was a tall, soft-spoken man who didn't say much and, at first it was difficult to ascertain his intentions. "There is so much spiritual confusion on this island; I would be hesitant to make an assessment with respect to God regarding what provokes her," he told my mother.

The seminary was crumbling with age and being ingulfed by the jungle, but it was still charming with its stone walls and cascading bougainvillea. The seminarians kept it clean, sweeping and washing the floors every day. They tilled the soil in the garden and pulled weeds. They hardly spoke to me at all and hardly spoke to each other; this I did not mind. The migraines had ceased and the wild beauty of the place inspired me to walk and explore the grounds, finding hidden statues of the saints and private shrines. I was permitted to explore and read the books in the library, journals of priests and nuns who documented their lives with God. It was in this library that I read for hours, at peace with the words of others. When I lived in the seminary, I did not dream. I slept soundly in the clean, ironed linens of my bed. School and friends and family, my father's lover, were all a part of an old life that I had cast aside.

Father Christophe spent mornings at the Lady in the Grotto, a statue of the Blessed Mother that had been positioned inside the carved stone of the mountain. Sometimes I would sit behind him, just out of sight and listen to him whisper the rosary amidst the chattering of bird calls. Once I found him cleaning up around her feet and went to help him. I saw what the peasants had left: coins, charms, bird bones, shells, flowers. "They play with me," he said, "leaving gifts for their *lwa Erzuli*. They leave the gifts at the feet of their deity, and I sweep them clean, in reverence of mine."

We visited the mountain peasants, bringing them food and clothes. They were appreciative and welcomed us into their humble homes made of mud with thatched roofs composed of palm leaves, where they offered us tea at their scrappy wooden tables and we saw the dark eyes of their children staring at us from the recesses of rooms, where candles and amulets and shrines of the *lwas* could be plainly seen. They placated Father Christophe, made him false promises about attending Bible study and mass. He gently chided them for their devotion to their *lwas*, telling them that only the risen Christ, the elevated soul, was worthy of their adoration. Afterward, he told me, he knew they were appeasing him. But they were hungry and must be fed. They were naked and must be clothed. "I can tell the story of the golden calf only so many times," he said. "I have to believe that actions speak louder than words."

As a way of repaying Father Christophe for his generosity, I wanted to cook a proper meal for Pentecost. Typically, the seminarians ate frugally and the food they prepared was simple and bland; I thought they deserved better for such a special day. My mother had learned the recipes of our family cook before we moved from the plantation, and she taught her daughters some of her favorite Creole meals. I went to market to buy the ingredients I needed.

There were trails through the forest down to the valley and a shortcut through the cemetery, but Father Christophe cautioned me not to go there, because this was where the *vodouisant* gathered and had their ceremonies. That day I took the wrong path back from market. I did not want to retrace my steps back and take the longer route, because I was plenty weary from the heat, so I kept my head down and walked quickly between the tombs. What I had entered was a strange kingdom, rows and rows of vine-covered mausoleums where goats and chickens roamed, where bones and amulets were nailed to trees and skulls hung from their branches. Worn shoes were placed aside the entrance of the tombs, cigarette butts and empty wine bottles strewn about everywhere.

I came to a place where there was water, a lagoon that surrounded a large tomb and there was a man swimming in it. When he came out, his hair glistened in the sun and he was completely naked but for an amulet about his neck. His skin was as black as midnight and the water droplets in his hair like constellations. He grabbed a blanket from a tree and dried himself with it. I crouched behind a tomb so he could not see me, but he called out. "I know you are there! And I know who you are!" Slowly, I peeked out from behind the tomb, curious. "You are Jean Louis's daughter. Do not worry. He is a good friend." He put on a white T-shirt and loose pants and motioned for me to go to him. "You need not be afraid, *Cheri*. Bathing with the bones of the dead brings luck and fortune," he said. "Your father and I swim here often." The water was clear and I could see the white walls of the submerged tomb. It rippled delicately in the breeze and seemed welcoming to me in the wretched heat.

"You too can go in if you like," the man said, motioning toward the water. He smiled a lot when he talked, as if he were self-assured and genuinely happy to be in my company. I clutched my bag of groceries and walked swiftly passed him. He called out, "I see you have gone to the market. What have you got there? Plantains? Beets? A baguette? Ah *Cheri*, this is quite a coincidence, don't you think? You and I meeting like this. It is not every day that I have the honor of meeting a beautiful *prix-des-yeux* like yourself."

I had not heard the term in quite a while, the one given by the *vodouisant* to those who have the "price of eyes"—the gift of clairvoyance. The man said his name was Papa Didi and that he had known my father since they were boys. He said that my father was good to honor his black grandmother in serving the *lwas* and that I should not judge him. He also said that I suffered headaches because the *lwas* were angry with me, because I did not use the gift they had given me for their purposes. "*Cheri*," Papa Didi said, "you are meant for us and you need to do good by the *lwas* or they will continue to punish you. Your father has told us about your headaches. He is worried about you."

"Your gods are demons," I said.

"They only mirror what is inside us," he said. "But yes, some of them are demons. And demons should be respected and kept happy."

I thought of Father Christophe and if he would be worried. I headed for another cemetery gate, but it was locked. I retraced my steps, running now, past Papa Didi, and he laughed as I passed him. I ran from tomb to tomb, my bag of groceries jostling against my ribs, trying to remember where I had come in, but it all looked the same. People were emerging now, from the cool of the tombs and moving into the light of the open grass. Beyond me, there was the rippling of sail cloth, and I saw women in white dresses and kerchiefs tying it to poles. The *vodouisant* gathered their offerings—chickens they carried by the feet, flapping and squawking. My heart was pounding in my ears as I saw them pass me by, carrying wine bottles and bougainvillea flowers, and boxes of cigars.

The pain had started again, and I felt weak; I panicked that I would not make it home. A woman approached me. She was very beautiful with waves of black hair down her back and flowers about her ankles. She took my hand. "Come, if you are thirsty, I will give you water."

I was wary of her, but desperately needed water, so I walked with her toward the tent.

"Come inside here," she said. "Here it is cool and you can rest."

Under the rippling sailcloth was a trickling fountain of water made of stone and moss. The woman filled a glass, gave it to me, and I readily drank it. She filled a porcelain bowl and washed her face and hands. Next to the fountain was a cot with a pillow. "It's okay," she said. "Please lie down. The heat has been dreadful."

I lay down on the cot, placed my head on the cool, soft pillow. Soon the world went blurry then dark. I must've slept for hours, because when I awoke, nightfall had come. Outside drums were beating and the *vodouisant* were singing. I made haste to the back of the tent by the fountain where there was an exit and then stopped; there was something moving along the moss. I scrambled back to the cot and watched as a snake carefully completed his descent over the rocks and to a bowl on the ground; he sniffed around it and then slithered out toward the jungle.

Suddenly, the voices and drumming stopped and there was the ringing of a bell. I peered out at the group and noticed a pale blue light. It wavered above the woman wearing flowers around her ankles; the white of her dress was gathered about her hips, her eyes were closed, her head thrown back. I heard the name again in my mind—*Martine*.

"You are free to go," said a familiar voice inside the tent. I turned around to see a man sitting amongst the flickering light of candles. "You passed out, Cheri. We wanted you to rest here."

He approached me, bent closer and I smelled the familiar aroma of rum intermixed with cologne—it was my father. Outside, the blue light was getting brighter. We both turned to look at it, as if it were a sunrise, something hopeful. My father bent and whispered softly in my ear: "Do you not feel it?"

I had felt it—joy. The *vodouisant* sang and danced and clapped their hands, and danced around each other laughing. Martine went to each of them and kissed them gently on the lips.

"Do you love her?" I asked my father.

"Of course!" he said. "I love everyone!"

He took my hand and led me out to the celebration where he danced and laughed and sang. I had not seen him that happy in a long time. He introduced me to the people, pride in his voice, and they gave me a hearty welcome. I recognized relatives, cousins and aunts and uncles I hadn't seen in ages, and they hugged me and pinched my cheeks. I cannot deny the feeling I had—it was if I had found a long-lost family. I had forgotten about the dinner, forgotten about Father Christophe. After a while, the blue light became paler and paler and the feeling of joy waned. Most of the people I knew left, as the drums beat more softly now and the crowd settled into a slower rhythm.

The dancing stopped and the fire burned fiercely in the night. Someone poured *clarin* on it and the flames leapt for the sky. Near the edge of the gate, the silhouettes of the palm trees bowed in the wind and the space between them took on a form. A strong wind rippled through the sail cloth. There was the breaking of glass and someone screamed—a high-pitched scream into the quiet night. One of the *kata* drummers, a young boy, dropped to the ground, writhing like a snake, his tongue flitting about, his scaly head shimmering in the light of the fire. My father looked out beyond the now smaller crowd gathered there, apprehension on his face.

In the light of the fire, I could see a figure stagger toward us. The firelight shone on the painted-on bones of his face and in the sheen of his top hat. Martine went to him and offered a mango and he bit it, and then he grabbed her wrist, pulled her to him, and kissed her hard on the mouth. When she resisted, he smacked her face so hard she fell down. "*Bouzen!*" He yelled. "Whore!"

He took a long sip of *clarin* and belched and hiccupped. "Oh that was jolly!" he said. "Jolly good!" and he leaned heavily on his cane as he limped toward us. Then he tripped and fell to the ground. A man helped him up and he pushed him away, "Get off me!" he said. He moved about the stragglers, lifting his hat and bowing and belching and stumbling until he came to me. "What have we here?" he said. "You are not one of the regulars!"

"Go gentle, *Guede*," my father said.

"Bah!" the man with the top hat said, and then he started laughing, a full bellied, drunken laugh. He gathered himself, "Why the long face, eh? Is something wrong? Have I offended you?" And then he raised his voice and it boomed in the darkness, "Have I offended you proud, soft-skinned mulatto *prix-des-yeux*! Hmmm? Am I not to your liking, *Cheri*? Hmmm? Are my clothes too soiled, my breath dank? Am I not HANDSOME?" And then he laughed, and the laugh became a wretched cough. He stumbled backward, caught himself. Then he marched right up to my face, and I looked into the stillness of his eyes and I saw decaying things, corpses, putrid flesh. I looked down and saw the bone-white amulet about his neck.

"What a brave one! She dares to look me in the eye! She dares to hold my gaze!" he shouted toward the crowd.

The drums began beating again, but this time it was a loud rumbling beat and the people danced around me, writhing and gyrating in ecstasy. They moved around me, grasping at me, clawing at my arms and legs, tearing my dress, their hot breath in my ears, on my skin. *Guede* unbuckled his belt from around his waist and slashed the air above me, I crouched, put my arms over my head. "Bow down!" he yelled. The dancers shouted nonsense in my ears as I cowered from the whip. "Bow down!" he yelled again. I braced myself for the strike of the whip, but it did not come. Then, everything went silent. When I raised my head to look around me, they were all gone. The dancers and drummers gone. My father and *Guede* gone. The tent—gone. Only the moon and the sky of stars and the silhouettes of tombs. "Papa!" I shouted and my voice echoed into the night. Above me the moon was setting in the sky and it lit up a path to a broken gate. I followed the moonlit path home.

I was no fool then, and I am no fool now. There was something in that water. I made up my mind then that I was not going to let anyone or anything manipulate me with respect to this power. I must figure it out on my own. From that point on, the headaches ceased.

I must tell you this: you and I, we are the sensitive ones, and when it is quiet, and when our minds are still, we are attuned to frequencies that go undetected by most. Try not to think too hard about what it all means. That's not for us to figure out. We are the ones whose job it is to wake others up. When this is done, the spirit will do its own work.

CHAPTER 4

VISITATION
NICOLETTA

That night just when I was about to drift off to sleep, the phone rang. It was Al. He said he was up from Florida to see his parents and he wanted to see Thomas. I reasoned he must be between girls. I tried not to badmouth my ex-husband in front of his son, and I was glad Thomas was too small to understand sarcasm, because a lot of the times that was how I alleviated the tension when I needed to deal with him. It killed me, however, to see how Al's selfish nature took advantage of Thomas, how he fit him in with a trip to see his parents, as if he wasn't special enough to warrant a trip himself. But that was Al, trying to kill two birds with one stone, so he would have more time for himself and whatever new babe he was entertaining.

"You'll have to drop him off," he said, "because I won't have a car, since both my parents are still working."

Years ago, I would have relented; I would have overextended myself for his sake, canceling plans and rearranging my day to accommodate him. I even, at one point, tried to win him back, by losing pounds jumping rope and doing Jane Fonda aerobics tapes. Thomas had just turned one and I had gained weight from the pregnancy. Also, I was pitying myself and felt guilty that we weren't a family, that Thomas didn't have a full-time dad. Al had turned forty, and I thought that he might have matured, that given this milestone, he might see the err of his selfish ways. I had to only show him that I could be as sexy as the other women he chased; that I would satisfy him, if he would satisfy me and the demands of a son. I wore tight jeans and low-cut blouses and won him back into my bed. But in the morning, he was up early, at the edge of the bed, putting on his socks, trying to sneak out. "I have plans. Going fishing with my stepfather on his new boat. And by the way, I'm moving to Florida. The fishing there is amazing."

There it was again "I" not "we." This was the letter that became ubiquitous and preceded the word divorce.

"I can't do that Al. I won't do that," I said in response to his not having a means of transportation.

"Whut," he said.

I repeated myself, annoyed. For a while now, Al had been losing his hearing, probably from hanging out late in bars and clubs where the music is loud and obnoxious. Al wasn't sophisticated enough to say "Pardon me?" or "I'm sorry?" He spits out a big, stupid *Whut* in your face. I stated my terms and he acquiesced to my demands. I heard the disappointment in his voice, as it disappeared into silence. But he didn't hang up. He waited for me to save him, deliver him from the disappointment, even if it was only a miniscule amount of what he dealt me. I grappled with myself in the silence, because there was another issue that was bothering me: now that my father was gone, who would take on that role for Thomas? Was this a small indication that Al was capable of change? I deduced that even if it was, making it easy for him wasn't the answer.

"I am sorry," I said. "Have a safe trip back."

I lay there in bed feeling the pang of disappointment again. And then I realized that my circles in life seemed petty compared to what Sabine had known, if it all was indeed true. What have I lived through, heartache, divorce? Other people's lives had legitimate tragedies. I thought of Sabine and her family losing everything, and the people who lived in the tombs, who lost everything. What have I known of this degree of pain? Just as I imposed the question on my mind, the phone rang again.

"Al, I am tired and I want to go to bed," I said, into the receiver. There was a silence and then, "Is this Nicoletta? This is Robert Kirton. We met a few weeks ago at the beach."

I was stunned: it was *him*. "Oh hello," I said.

"I've done some sleuthing to find your number. I am sorry for calling so late. But I was wondering, could we... could we meet at the beach this Saturday afternoon?"

"Sure," I said, trying to hide the emotion in my voice. "What time would you like to meet?"

"How about 2 pm at the bench where we met?"

"That would be fine."

"Okay. Thanks. Thank you. I will see you then. Have a good night."

"Good night."

I hung up the phone and felt ecstatic and fantasized of having the priest in my bed, loving him and him loving me until I couldn't stand the vibration any longer, reached between my legs and alleviated all tension, then drank a glass of wine and took a pill to knock myself out.

It was a brisk, October day when I met Robert Kirton—Father Kirton—at the beach. I went early to compose myself. I was anxious but excited as well, and my excitement seem to overrule my obsession with the sensation of panic. I sat in the car and watched the seagulls standing in a group in the parking lot, aligning themselves with the wind. I got out of the car and walked toward the boardwalk, to the bench where I met Robert Kirton a few weeks ago. There were fewer people here than when we had first met, and now they were wearing jackets and sweatshirts. There was a man with a metal detector scanning the sand for summer's lost trinkets. I closed my eyes and tried again, as I did last night and the night before, remembering what Sabine had said, how the mind must be calm to conjure up the woman, my doppelganger, the woman that this Robert Kirton had loved. But there was nothing.

Robert Kirton appeared then, near the beach house, his hands in his jacket pockets. He was not dressed in black, nor wearing the collar. He turned in my direction and stopped, recognizing me, and I thought to myself, why on Earth do I have such intimate knowledge of this man's life and just how do I fit into the equation?

We walked for a while along the shoreline and Robert periodically picked up a shell and examined it. "I collect these, keep them in my pocket, and take them out, turn them over between my fingers; such small, smooth things are good for rumination." And he handed me the shell, white and smooth with a small fold where a creature once lived. We continued walking, without either one of us saying why we were there, toward the bluffs—sand cliffs of precarious heights that were under rolling gray clouds miles away—a place that seemed treacherous and forbidden.

"I can't stop thinking about what you said. About your... vision. The church warns about premonitions; such visions, they say, are always from nefarious sources. But I don't think I believe that."

He stopped when he said this, and I suddenly became self-conscious, like I couldn't bear him to look at me. It was all so strange, battling my inner fantasies and needs, my insecurities, and the will to please him, to say something that would keep him coming back. The clouds usurped the sun now, and the wind was blowing harder. There were white caps on the waves and people were moving toward the parking lot.

"What do you believe?" I asked.

"I struggle with that question every day with respect to all sorts of things."

It was an honest statement, and one I wouldn't think uttered by a priest. But then again, there was nothing about him that indicated he *was* a priest. He wore jeans and loafers, a non-descript wind-breaker, was clean shaven, and had a slight scent of cologne, but nothing too overbearing. It was a hint, a light scent on the skin or face that gave away a particular sensuality. It was electrifying to be near him.

"Oh, how nefarious could this be if Florence is your mother! She is quite a lady. Very devout, very kind. Did you know that she brings over food for us sometimes?"

"No," I said. "That's a new one." Apparently, the president of the Marion Legion and I weren't the only ones looking to make an impression on Robert.

"I'm sorry about your father, by the way. I didn't know him, but I remember his funeral. He was a man who was certainly loved."

The line of friends and family down the street at his funeral was evidence of this, and the image of it appeared in my mind. The mere mention of my father forced me to consider it—how the outcome of this relationship was not something that concerned me alone. There were others involved—my mother, which was a bit laughable, and then Thomas and his needs, and how this might affect him. This is what my father would consider first and foremost: how others—his children—were affected by his actions.

"He was loved. He was a good man. He wasn't easy to get along with sometimes, but you knew he loved you."

Suddenly he stopped. "Nicoletta… Nicky. I called you here… because I need to know— I mean, I'm sure you are wondering—I called you, because I want to ask you if there was anything else about my fiancé, anything else that might have come through—that you can tell me."

"Did you tell me her name?" I tried to prolong the issue, divert where the conversation was going. Maybe it would still happen; maybe it would happen now.

"I may have. Elena is—was—her name."

I turned the shell over and over between my fingers.

"There hasn't been anything else?"

"I'm sorry. It must've been a fluke."

"This is not something that happens regularly?"

"No. Not regularly. Definitely not regularly."

"Okay," he said, and looked out toward the bluffs, nodding his head.

"But maybe there is a way. I can consult with someone—someone who knows more about these things than I do. She is a clairvoyant. A *bona fide* clairvoyant."

"I appreciate that," he said, "but, I might have to admit to myself that maybe this isn't what I thought it was—. What I hoped it was."

"What did you think it was?"

"Let's walk back," he said. "It's getting cold."

"No, wait."

He looked at me and I saw the grief in his face, the skepticism was moving in.

"An answer. I thought it might be a means to an answer."

"Maybe it is. Let me help you," I said. "Give me the chance."

I was attempting to rein him back in, for my sake, not his. I was fully aware of that. What I couldn't rightly articulate, however, was *why*. *Why* was I so enamored with this completely unavailable man?

He looked down at his feet. "Goodness, it is getting cold all of a sudden."

"I feel like a failure," I said.

"No," he said. "Let's try it. I will give you some time. Maybe there will be more insights. There's nothing to lose, right? Except—please, may I have your confidence in this. Please, I trust you. This is between us."

"Yes, of course."

We walked back to the parking lot, our hands in our jacket pockets, trying to protect them from becoming raw from the wind. We went toward the beach house where the wind wasn't as strong. I saw it then, recognized it—despondency; it was in the shape of his face, his mouth drawn down, his eyes following some imaginary line on the ground, looking but not seeing.

"When I got the transfer here to St. Anthony's, I thought it was a new start. I felt like it was possible—I could move on. I started to. I would come here, walk the beach, pray; walking by the water and praying was cathartic. But this, and you, and… I'm sorry. I don't know why I am telling you this. I shouldn't be telling you this and expecting something from you. That's not fair."

"No. No, don't say that. This is definitely a weird situation. And I want to help you. I really do."

"I know you do. You're a kind person; I see that. But this is a bit cruel. Fate's little joke. I'm not strong enough to not question, to not pursue this. I should be, but I'm not."

"Who would be strong enough not to pursue this? Who would be satisfied with not knowing?"

"People with sufficient faith. I should be one of those people. Someone who can pass the test."

I thought of the letter that I had found earlier that was surely written by him, the letter that said, "Forgive me."

"Is that what you think this is, a test?"

"It has all the elements of a test. I've never thought the God I believed in was that sort of Old Testament God—the patriarchal God who asked Abraham to put the knife to Isaac's throat. That God."

We reached his car and he took his keys from his pocket. I worried then, if I was ever going to see him again, if he would drop off the face of the earth, like other men. He opened the car door and then faced me, his dangerously blue eyes looking deeply into me. The wind screeched through the eaves of the beach house, an ominous sound.

"It really is uncanny," he said, and then got into his car and drove away.

As I watched the car become smaller and drive away out of sight, a word formed inside of me: *capable*. He made me feel *capable*, and I was determined to prove him right.

It was a week after that I went to Sabine to inquire of her help.

"Contacting the dead?" she asked, chuckling. "There is no contacting the dead! This the trickery of charlatans. You don't contact the dead. They contact you. You are sent—information—when your mind is still. That is the best we can do. So, the first thing, as we discussed before, is to steady the mind."

That must've been it. My mind wasn't steady; it's never been steady, only in certain moments, like just before sleep, or in deep dreams, or in moments where I forget myself and become a part of the environment, like at the beach. But to do it here, on call, seemed impossible.

Sabine learned to meditate from a fellow clairvoyant, who learned it from a practicing Buddhist. She had me sit on a pillow on the floor with my legs crossed. She told me to follow the rhythm of my breath as it went in and out of my body. We were the only two in the store: my mother had Thomas and Esmerelda was somewhere else. So, I sat and tried to follow my breath, but instead, I tried to control it, which made me tense. Then I thought about what I could make for dinner. Or how I wanted chocolate, or how heavy my body was from lack of quality sleep. I tried to focus on the falling water of the fountain, but then I wanted to pee. Most prevalent, however, were thoughts of Kirton, and how I wanted to see him again. Just thinking of him sent a buzz throughout my body that was more like an annoyance, unsettling, a drug of some sort that was only recently injected.

"I can't do it. My mind is too active. Too concerned with—garbage. Chores. What I will have for dinner. Stupid things."

"Yes, of course that is all there. But beyond that is a stillness. The breath will lead you there."

"I have a hard time believing that. I can't just notice my breath, follow it. It becomes yet another thing I try to force and make right."

Sabine closed her eyes, to follow her breath to stillness, and she seemed the picture of peace, perfectly attuned to her inner life. I wondered how long it took, how many years of practicing to calm her mind. My mind was like a toddler that needed a toy, or a dog that needed a treat, here have this to play with, shut up now and do what I tell you. But Sabine had already come through all that. She was a model, a future self, I'd like to think, of who I could become if only I would evolve.

As I walked back to my car, it started to rain, the cold, autumn rain of a godless night. The harbor was out there, bearing witness, and it seemed a palatable transference of angst, of all the suffering souls whose needs remain unfulfilled. This fantasy of mine was yet another thing that would go unfulfilled, and I thought of the time Carmen and I had tried to build an amusement park in the backyard: I had envisioned trapezes hanging from the trees, and a mini roller coaster, and how we could charge people a fee to run it and the entire neighborhood would come and enjoy our park. We told my mother and she scoffed at us, told us to set up a lemonade stand instead, and with each passing day, the idea became less and less a possibility until we realized that it was ridiculous: we were just kids who had no resources to make such a thing come to fruition.

I started the car and turned on the wipers and a dampness passed through my body. It occurred to me then that I was missing something: I was so intent on pleasing Robert and getting closer to him by way of his dead fiancé, that I never asked what it was that he wanted to know. What had died with her; what remained unanswered?

My mother calls me up on the phone, "What are you and Thomas doing for dinner? I've made a roast. Come over. There will be enough for the three of us."

"Really? Okay."

"How come you haven't called? Are you sick?"

"No. Not sick," I said. "Just busy, I guess."

It was a lie. I wasn't busy. I just didn't want to tie up the phone, thinking he would call and get a busy signal and that would deter him. Every time the phone rang, it was torture. Do I let it ring and not seem eager and desperate? It was all absurd, the fact that I was thinking this way about a priest. But I could not deny—that night I last saw him two weeks ago—there was a connection between us, and it wasn't just *her*. Also, I didn't need my mother sniffing around this relationship, curious as to what was bothering me. But she came right out and called, even though it's not her way. She usually waits for me to call her, because she feels it's more my place to call than hers. She has always had her pride, and this makes her even more cryptic, the predominant attribute that drove my father crazy. Ma, are you mad? No, I'm not mad. Ma, are you hurt? No, of course I'm not hurt. Ma, are you scared? Who me? What do I have to be afraid of? I have this theory that when I passed through my mother's body, I took all of her emotion from her—the torrent of anger, the abyss of fear, the well of sadness.

"Not sick. Well, okay, you don't have to come if you don't want to. I just thought I'd save you a night of cooking."

Guilt trip. Not, oh Nicoletta, I'd like to see you. I just thought I'd save you a night of cooking, she says.

"What time do you want us over?

We pulled in the driveway and it was already dark at 5 pm; the lights were on in the front of the church, the street lamp shown down on Robert's car—the car I recognized from the beach. This would be a tantalizing night, the fact that he was near, but that I could not visit him, because my mother would ask questions.

I lifted Thomas up to ring the doorbell. Every time my mother answers the front door to let me in, I find myself in wonderment at how small she's gotten.

"Hello, dollface! Guess what! I got something for you. Hey, dollface, I got something for you. I bought you a truck." She bent down and put the toy truck on the floor and gave it a push. "Zoom!" she said as the truck whizzed across the floor. Thomas ran gleefully after it and I bent to kiss my mother. Usually, I give her a small peck on the check and we're done with it. But this time, she reached her gnarled fingers up to my face, cupping my chin. I sank so easily and stayed there in my mother's arms for a moment. She started to laugh a little.

"What's the matter, doll?" she asked.

My mother hasn't called me doll in years. I sank a little more, wanting comfort from her.

"Nothing. Nothing's wrong."

"It doesn't look like nothing's wrong."

"I'm tired," I said, my excuse for everything.

"Well, sit down and rest."

She went to the stove and put her oven mitt on. "Boy, this is a perfect night for a roast. So damp out there. And the early darkness is just so hard this time of year."

My mother's house was hot and stifling. I was agitated enough, so I went to the window, disconnected the alarm, and threw open the sash. A small breeze moved in and tossed at her lace curtains.

My father bought the alarm system after they had a break-in when they were in Florida. It was yet another indication that the neighborhood was changing, becoming more city-like, with a stoplight on every corner, traffic, stores where farmland had been. I remember my mother at the window looking out at the meadow behind our house, lamenting to herself why she agreed to leave the city and her family and move to the middle of nowhere. I, on the other hand, felt right at home. My sister and I would lay in the hammock in the summer and gaze at the multitude of stars overhead, listening to the crickets. There was a peace to life back then, be it the simplicity of childhood or the simplicity of the land, that soothed me. Now there are traffic lights everywhere, cars are ubiquitous, and sirens go off constantly. My mother, however, seems to be fine with it all.

I moved about the house, in and out of all of the empty and altered rooms devoid of our belongings. Now even my father's things have been given away. The furniture is stale, the décor dated, and I am pressed to admit, with the splash over air across my face, that I go about the place living on two levels simultaneously: on one level, there is grief, and the ghosts of the past. The lively place that was once my family's home where we loved, fought, and lived the day-to-day was now only a shell in which my mother could live out her days. On the other level, my job as a daughter was to be present for her and listen to her, to her stories, the gossip, the complaining, despite the ever-present feeling of inadequacy that I had not done what she expected of me to stay married and have the family she had. But now what overshadowed these two levels of awareness was a third, more prominent level. I was guilty. I was guilty because I was hiding something.

I circled back and put my purse on the dining room table and turned to go back into the kitchen, when something caught my eye. It was a picture on the dining room server amongst all the different family photos of my brother, sister and me at different stages in our lives; the grandchildren at milestone events, birthdays, baptisms, Christmas, and Easter. The picture was of a priest—the garb was apparent from a few feet away. When I went closer and took the photo in my hands, I saw that it was a picture of Robert with his hair parted ridiculously to the side and plastered in place. He was younger and the picture was awkward and amateurish, a photo that reminded me of the numerous school pictures I had taken in my life. Was I seeing things? Was this a hallucination? Was I really losing my mind? I looked at my mother who had her back to me, pouring gravy over the roast.

"Ma, why do you have this picture of this... priest?"

"What?"

"The priest. Father, um, what's-his-name. Why on Earth do you have his photo?"

"Oh that. He gave it to me."

"Why?"

"Because we are praying for one another."

She faces me now, her gold necklace of the Virgin and the Christ Child resting prominently on her protruding breastbone. My mother has a high breastbone, like a proud falcon, staking out the land from high atop a tree.

"You are praying for one another."

"Yes. At our last Marion Legion meeting the President gave us all an assignment, to pray for one another and she split us up into twos and Father Kirton and I were matched."

"But why the picture?"

"Because when you are praying for someone, you should look at their face. I gave him a picture of me, too. Listen. Do you want just peas and carrots, or should I make a salad?"

I set the photo back down. Then, it occurred to me how absurd it all was. I burst out laughing. I laughed until tears came out of my eyes, at Robert's ridiculous expression mismatched with my mother's piety and her complete ignorance of how I too had a thing for this man.

"*What* is so funny?"

"It's such a stupid picture. I'm ... sorry... but it's such a stupid picture..."

"It is not stupid. *Jeezis*, what is wrong with you. I think you are cracking up."

"Ha ha ha. Yeah. Maybe. It certainly does seem that way, doesn't it. Ha ha ha ha ha."

Thomas, now on the floor by the refrigerator, looked at me and clapped his hands.

"Mommy is nuts, isn't she. Come on now, Nicky, get a hold of yourself and come and eat."

My mother put Thomas in his booster seat and put a few pieces of beef and some carrots on his tray. I sat down, still trying to stifle my laughter. She made our plates; I didn't have much of an appetite, but I knew if I didn't eat something, she'd start suspecting something, so I shoveled food into my mouth just to get it down.

"I have something to tell you," she said.

I put down my knife and fork. "Oh God. What?"

"It's nothing! Don't be so uptight. It's just something a little strange, that's all."

"What. What's strange."

"It's your father. I think he's still in the house," my mother said while she nonchalantly cut up her meat.

"What do you mean he's still in the house?"

"I mean, I think he never left. I saw him just this past Monday. I got up earlier than usual, because I had this feeling that someone was in the house, and I saw your father at the foot of the bed, looking out the side window."

"You must've been dreaming."

"No. No, I was awake. I am sure of it. First, I thought maybe it was a hallucination. They changed my blood pressure medication again, and sometimes it makes me feel strange, but then I was doing the dishes this morning, and I felt a slap across my behind. Just like that—a slap. Your father used to do that sometimes, you know, in a kidding way. Playfully."

"A slap—"

"Yeah."

"And what does um, the priest say about this situation: Daddy's ghost slapping your behind?"

"I haven't told him. But I felt like I have to tell somebody. So, I told you."

"Are you going to tell Bardo?"

"Probably not. He'll think I'm crazy."

"So you tell me because you think I'm crazy and I can sympathize?"

"I didn't say that."

"I'm sure this is typical for someone who is grieving," I said.

"You don't believe me, do you."

"I don't know what to believe."

With that the reality of the situation hit me. Robert and my mother *were* perfect for one another.

We cleaned up the dishes and my mother fed Thomas a bowl of ice cream. Thomas made the *mmmm mmmm* sounds that he makes when he really loves what he is eating. I finally could escape the table and peer out across the street. If the car was there, I would go to him. If the car was there, I would say I needed to go to the drugstore to pick something up, that I needed air and I would go to him. Surely,

I could think up some reasonable excuse on a night like tonight. But when I looked toward the parking lot, the car was gone.

CHAPTER 5

PRESENT DAY PRODIGAL SON
BARDO

Bardo pulled into the driveway, shut the car off and sat there as the dread swarmed his mind. He closed his eyes and tried to compose himself only to feel the last of the heat leak from the car. It was beyond dusk and the world around him was frozen again. Footsteps across the street were snapping on the sidewalk, dark figures walking to the Saturday evening mass. He grabbed the jug of wine in the passenger's seat, opened the door, and stepped into the cold night.

When Bardo opened the front door, he saw his mother at the sink washing dishes. She turned around, looked at him, and grabbed a towel to wipe her hands.

"Oh good. You're here."

"Hello, Mother," he said, bending down to kiss the top of her head. Every year she seemed to get smaller and bending to kiss her on the cheek was almost awkward, so he took to kissing her on the top of her head, as if she were a child. He placed the wine he brought on the table.

"Come on, sit down. I got pork chops and escarole and beans cooking. We'll eat first and then you can shave him. He's sleeping now."

"Okay."

Florence had the table set for two, complete with a fresh tablecloth and basket of Italian bread. Bardo went to the table and helped himself to a glass of wine. The garlic aroma stimulated his hunger, so he grabbed a piece of bread, sliced it open, and buttered it generously.

"How is he?" he asked.

Florence put both hands on the counter and stared out the kitchen window at the night coming in over the vacant lot behind the house. She gave in a little, and Bardo could hear her whimper. His mother was not a person who cried often and when she did, it was awkward. He got up and went to her and tried to embrace her, but she wriggled away from him and went to the stove. She reached for the oven mitt, fetched the pork chops from the broiler, and put them on the top of the stove.

"Give me your bowl," she said. "I'll give you some escarole."

Bardo fetched the bowl from his place setting and handed it to his mother and then went to sit at the table.

"What do you think, more?" she asked, showing him the serving in his bowl.

"Yeah, a little more."

Florence ladled some more and placed the bowl in front of him.

"Ma, would you like me to pour you some wine?"

"Yeah, okay." Florence went to her place setting and grabbed her napkin. "Here, give me your dish. I will give you a pork chop."

Bardo handed his mother his dish.

Florence loaded Bardo's plate with two large pork chops and made herself a small bowl of escarole and beans.

"Is that all you're eating?" he asked her.

"I'm not hungry," she said. She rose, went to the oven and shut it off. "Jesus, it's hot in here," she said, sitting back down. "How is Regina?" Florence asked, changing the subject.

"I don't know."

"What do you mean you don't know."

"We've decided to take a break for a while."

"Now?"

Bardo swirled a piece of bread in his escarole, sopping up the oil and broth, wondering how he could divert the conversation.

"She's a nice girl, Bardo. She treats you right. You need someone like her right now."

"C'mon Ma, we're not going to get into this, are we?"

"With all that studying about how to be a shrink, couldn't you figure out what your problem is? I don't want to die knowing you're going to be all alone in the world."

"I'm not alone, Ma."

"Yeah, no kidding you're not alone," Florence said under her breath.

Bardo ate the bread with the oil and it was good. He took a knife to the pork chop and sliced to see if it was dry. "Are you insinuating that I don't know loneliness?"

"I'm insinuating that Regina would be a good wife."

"I can't commit to her."

"You can't commit to anyone," Florence said, shaking her head. She poured herself a glass of wine. "This wine is cheap," she said. "Why do you get me this rosé? It tastes like water."

"You told me to get Gallo. Any kind of Gallo. That's what you said. You should have told me you don't like rosé."

"I don't like rosé. Get me good red wine."

Florence took a sip of the wine and made a face, like it was sour.

"So, what did you tell Regina?"

"Mom, I never promise them anything. Right from the start they know what they are getting into with me."

"You say one thing and do another. That's the problem. When it comes down to deciding what's what, they see it how they want to see it. Take another pork chop. Here, they're small."

Bardo handed his dish over willingly.

"I'll tell you what you do wrong. You bring them into the family and they start to think they belong, and then everything gets screwed up, because we start to treat them like they belong."

He cut into his pork chop and took a bite. It was delicious. None of the women he dated could cook like his mother.

"Yes, everything gets screwed up. That's right," he said, irritated.

"Don't bring them here anymore."

"Okay, I won't."

He thought of last Wednesday when Cheryl came in with her big leather boots and fed him an ice cream cake in the back room, bit by bit, scraping at the cream with her long nails. The sex was delectable and primal and wonderfully spontaneous. But he felt a certain amount of repugnance for himself when he argued with his mother or father about not wanting a wife.

Bardo and his mother ate the rest of the meal in silence. They were both tired. Afterward, Bardo went up to his father's room, feeling the anxiety tighten in his chest. He thought he convinced himself that he was prepared for what was to come, but the closed bedroom door seemed like a wall. He was hesitant; touched the metal of the doorknob, peered at the ghastly face in the grain of the door that he had known for years. His mother came up behind him, and he turned the doorknob. It was completely dark inside. He listened closely for his father's breathing and thought for a second there was no sound. The dread intensified. "Dad…" he called out, panicked. He went forward into the darkness of the room.

There was a tussling of the sheets and a heavy sigh. Bardo's dread drained away.

"Bardo," Dante said in a scratchy voice. "How you doin' son?"

"I'm fine, Dad. Do you want to sleep some more? I can come back. I'm sorry I woke you."

"No, no. Been sleeping enough. Turn on the light."

Bardo hesitated before he flicked the switch. Annoyed with his cowardice, he turned on the light and faced his father. He could see the shape of Dante's large skull; his eyes seemed smaller now, sunken in their large sockets. Bardo was horrified at the sight of him, how thin he was but forced himself to look into his eyes to find the place his father retreated to inside the emaciated figure.

His father now had the king size bed all to himself. Bardo remembered lying next to his mother in this same bed, when his father got up to go and get the morning paper, feeling the warmth of her body under the covers and being at ease with himself and the world, until his father came into the room and yelled at him that he didn't belong in this bed, curled up next to his mother. He was getting too old for such things.

His father cleared his throat and sat up straight. Florence brought in the bowl of water and the shaving cream and positioned it on the table. They joked about the pieces of tissue paper Bardo often had on his face after shaving. His father chuckled a little and the tension lessened. Bardo sprayed the shaving cream into his hand and smoothed it over his father's face. It was awkward at first to be so near his father, but his father closed his eyes and Bardo relaxed. Bardo carefully maneuvered the razor around Dante's chin and then cleaned the razor in the water. He moved the razor gently down his father's neck, and Dante breathed a long sigh. Bardo interpreted this as yet another surrender; it was a practice that was still new to his father—the relinquishing of power. Bardo wanted his father to see that he would not cut him, that he could do it neatly; that he could do it right.

Afterward, his father looked fresh and more alive. Bardo wondered if this would be the last time he would see him, and he thought it might be good, with his father's face looking like it did—composed. But then the reality of his father's life being final, came with a blow: a memory rushed in then to spoil the moment. He remembered how the headlights of the car came barreling through the night. It was the same car Bardo used to take Gretchen to the clinic to get an abortion just a few days before, unbeknownst to his father. He remembered the disappointment in his father's voice when he got in the car, about the hippies and the marijuana, and the possibility of getting caught again. The abortion loomed in his mind then; it made the pot seem petty and insignificant. What would his father have said if he knew? Why couldn't he have been a better son? Bardo's throat began to ache with tension; the pain was all localized there, where his voice was. Then he felt his father grab hold of his wrist; it was a strong, fortifying grasp. Bardo realized then that there was no need for words now. There were always words before and they were never right. The grasp of his father's big hand was enough.

That night, Bardo showed up at Regina's apartment. Regina was curled in a comforter on her couch preparing her lecture when the doorbell rang. She quickly deduced it was her neighbor Bev, bringing over the mail that was erroneously placed in her box. Regina lingered, finished scribbling a thought, and the doorbell rang again, several times. She got up, frustrated from being disturbed, peeked through the tiny glass hole in her door and saw Bardo's warped head. *Oh for Chrissakes*, she mumbled. Her brain jammed with all of the scenarios she conjured up in her spare time, how she would handle such a situation. She looked again; this time his nose grew to the size of a small branch off his face. She opened the door.

"What do you want, Bardo?"

"Hi," Bardo said.

He stood there and regarded her with what seemed to be anticipation and expectation; he wanted to be let in. She watched his breath appear in front of his mouth, move like a cloud away from his face and dissipate into the night.

"Can I come in?" he asked, almost annoyed.

"Why," she said.

"Why not," he answered.

"Plenty of reasons," she said.

He looked up at the night sky; the clouds drifting like specters, phantoms, dreams. He blinked his eyes, "Why do you have to be like this," he said.

Regina was furious with him for being so selfish, but at the same time, she knew the grief he was facing. Her empathy allowed for vulnerability and surrender and she opened the door.

"I'm only going to stay a few minutes," he said.

She went to her small wooden kitchen table and sat down. He pulled up a chair and sat across from her. So many mornings they both sat here after a night of love, eating pancakes or strudel or whatever Regina fancied to make him that morning. He always complimented her on the coffee and the fresh fruit; he ate like he was a king. Regina always did her best to dazzle him with food. She knew his mother was a good cook and his expectations were high.

They met in college in a Sociology class. Regina was smart and studious, but she drank too much, mostly to alleviate her stress. Bardo asked Regina to help him study for a test, which at first was a pretense for sleeping together; but they soon discovered that they could work well together and help each other. Regina took meticulous notes; Bardo could make sense of abstract theories and relate them to her in common terms. They were friends and lovers, and Regina pretended to keep it light, despite her feelings for him, because she knew he was a man who liked women and women liked him. After college, Regina left and went to grad school in Boston; she extricated herself from the relationship—it was a ploy to get him to realize how much he loved her. But Bardo never called, and he never showed up unannounced, like she dreamed he'd do. After graduation, she worked as an adjunct, then an associate professor for ten years until her mother fell ill with breast cancer and she came home to be with her.

It was a bad time. She didn't have a job, drank a lot, and found herself hanging around with friends she went to high school with, friends who were now alcoholics themselves or drug addicts, people with no ambition for life. She ran into Bardo at a bar and they took up where they left off.

Bardo sat down, thinking about what Regina was wearing, the soft robe with its loose tie, the V-neck of her pajamas showing the constellation of freckles just under her collarbone. But he didn't come tonight to kiss the constellation of freckles. Or at least this is what he told himself. He came because he needed a friend and Regina had always been that—a friend. He stared at the place where the wood planks were glued together to make her table, as he had done so many times before, and at the remnants of food stuck permanently in the interstices.

"Would you like a cup of tea?" Regina asked to fill the silence.

"Sure, that would be great."

She rose and filled the kettle with water, retrieved the Earl Grey from the cabinet, set the kettle on the stove, and turned on the flame. It ticked too long before lighting and the gas smell filled the room.

"Damn," he said. "Someday you're going to blow this place up."

Regina ignored the comment, placed the tea bag in a cup, and looked at Bardo, who was still staring at the crumbs in the interstices of the table.

"He's going to die soon," he said and rubbed his eyes.

Bardo was trying to pull her back in emotionally, and she needed to stand her ground. Show him that she was moving on, despite this ploy for attention. Despite the fine way he looked in those jeans and the way he smelled of clean soap and licorice, and the scruff of his unshaven beard, which had always excited her in a primal way. *The Feminist's Response to Freud*, she said, muttering the name of her dissertation under her breath. *The Feminist's Response to Freud*. She went to grab her own teacup from the living room where she was studying, returned and pulled the whistling kettle from the stove. With a soft hush of water and steam, she filled his cup and then handed it to him. She hung back at the counter to be as far away from him as she could while still being courteous.

"Would you mind if I helped myself to some milk and sugar?"

Regina blushed. She had forgotten the condiments. "You know where they are," she said, trying to be cool.

Bardo stood up and took off his jacket, placed it around the back of his chair. He went to the counter and fetched the sugar bowl, and a spoon from the drying rack, and the milk from the fridge. She watched him as he fixed his tea, and she did her best to suppress the feelings of joy that were rising in her breast from seeing him at last after so many weeks.

"Aren't you going to sit down?" he asked.

"I'm fine where I am," she said.

Bardo wrung his tea bag against the side of his cup with his spoon, then placed it on a napkin. "So how are you?" he asked her.

"I'm fine," she said.

"You hate me, don't you?"

"I don't hate you."

Bardo brought the tea to his mouth and placed it back down when he felt the heat of the cup. "Can you please just be my friend right now? You, more than anyone, know how this works."

"Bardo, I am truly sorry about your father, but I think you are selfish in what you are asking of me."

Regina watched Bardo's face change as she spoke. His thick, black eyebrows crinkled.

"Why must you get all caught up in the romantic tragedy thing. We've always seen eye-to-eye with one another. Why can't that continue?"

"Because it can't. Because you hurt me. Because you want to fuck other people."

"My father is dying. I have to see him turn into this emaciated monster with a tumor the size of a basketball in his belly. Do you really think my mind is on fucking anyone?"

"Yes. Yes, I do," she said. "Because that is how you're wired. It's quintessential Freud: sex is everything for you."

Bardo waved his hand at her. "That's a bunch of bullshit," he said in anger.

Regina huddled about her cup, sipped, quietly cowering at the intensity of the feeling radiating across the room. It was obvious: he was feeling pain now too, and Regina wondered whose pain would win.

She thought of the day they went to a mutual college friend's birthday party in upstate New York. She had just completed the AA program and decided to finish her dissertation; all was good: it was a beautiful fall day and they stopped at a wine and cheese shop for Pellegrino and a block of cheese and a baguette and a roll of salami and they pulled off the main road onto a dirt road and lay down a blanket and drank the water and ate the cheese and the salami, and she sat stroking his hair as they both watched the shimmering trees lose their leaves in the warm sun, and it was something wonderful, something ephemeral and sublime the way the gold of the leaves shimmered and floated delicately down. "I love being with you," Bardo said. And she felt wonderfully alive; they shared that aliveness with each other, at the cusp of the seasons, and this is when Regina thought that it was possible, that she could convert him into someone who could love her, and only her, for a lifetime.

Sitting at the table, Bardo recalled that same autumn day in the warm sun watching the leaves fall and lying with his head in Regina's lap as she stroked his temples, tracing his hair line, running her fingers through his mass of curls, and he thought of his mother, how she would stroke his temple at night to soothe him, and he felt soothed and happy that the anxiety and angst that had become prominent after graduation had retreated for the time being, that he could still feel joy.

Bardo suddenly stood up. Regina's heart sank: he was leaving. "I need to use your bathroom," he said. She sighed with relief. "You know where to find it," she said, staring at his rear end as he walked down the hall.

She could not deny that she was thrilled to see him. It took an enormous amount of energy to conjure up the façade of anger and suppress the need to wrap her arms around him, to feel that familiar warmth. She rose from the table to put the milk in the refrigerator, working the metrics in her mind of how she could turn things around. She shut the refrigerator door, and he returned. She turned to face him and that's when she noticed his fly. It was open, all the way down. Bardo saw Regina staring and then he looked down too. The two of them stood opposite one another, staring at Bardo's open fly, as if it would suddenly start to talk and instruct them on what to do.

"*Oh Jeezis*," Bardo said.

Bardo attempted to zip himself up, but the zipper wouldn't move. He turned to face the wall. "I think it's stuck," he said. "It's jammed."

"You're fooling; it is not."

"I'm not kidding." He threw up his hands in futility and turned around. "Whatever," he said.

Regina looked carefully at the fly. "It seems like it's caught on your boxers."

Bardo looked down at himself again and laughed. Regina laughed too. Then he stopped and looked at her with that pleading face of his. He walked toward her.

Regina stared at the tea in her cup, still steaming with the water from the kettle, still hot. She tried to hide her smile. She cowered, turned away from him. Bardo stood behind her now. He put his hands on her shoulders. "You're strong," he said. "You've always been strong." Regina softened with the touch. She turned around. Bardo cupped his hands under her chin. She closed her eyes. "Please," he said, "please." He embraced her. They held each other. Then Bardo started to stroke her back, her hair. It felt so good to have him touch her again; it was like a drug in her veins. *Yes,* she thought, happy he wanted her. *Yes, yes, yes. No,* her mother said inside her head. *You give it away and he will waste it. Be the Madonna, not the whore. The Feminist's Response to Freud.* Bardo was stroking her breast with his thumb now. It was such a brazen thing to do. "No," she said, and pushed him away. "No, you can't do that anymore."

"I'm sorry," he said and backed away, palms in the air. "I'm sorry. That wasn't my intention." Bardo ran his fingers through his hair. He sat back down. "Do you want me to leave?"

"Yes," she said, lying. "Yes. Get out."

She thought of the leaves again and the gilded trees. They would all be bare now. What was the use? Regina's throat painfully ached with the words she trapped there. Bardo grabbed his coat and put his arms in the sleeves, slowly, waiting for her to change her mind. He went to the door, opened it and left.

Regina watched as the headlights of his car illuminated the trees and then pulled away, leaving nothing but the lonesome night outside her window.

Months after his father died, Bardo's mother called him one night and told him that she wanted to sell the Grand Prix. Her doctor told her that she should no longer drive because of her glaucoma and she told Bardo that if he sold the car, he could keep the money, so long as he drove her where she needed to go if she could not take the bus or the train.

As a little boy, Bartholomew used to sit in the back seat of his father's Grand Prix and fill the rim of his father's hat with tiny balls of paper so that when he drove, it snowed. On the long drives to his grandmother's house in Westbury, he could feel the way the Grand Prix responded to the Northern State Parkway, the way its wheels thumped over the joints in the concrete in a mesmerizing cadence. The man behind the wheel never said too much when he drove; Bardo supposed he liked what it did to his thinking, how the thoughts and the music and the movement produced a pleasant momentum that allowed one to transcend the problems of life, at least for the time being. His father was a thinker, like he was a thinker; like Bardo, he had a big brain and a little life, a relatively uneventful, typical, monotonous life, and this combination brought anxiety and angst. Bardo knew this all too well, and he recognized it in his father his senior year in college when his father left the lawn mower on the front lawn and hopped a plane to Florida to escape from the routine-less life of retirement.

Bardo also recognized, that for the most part, his father disciplined himself to live within the confines of a humble life. He thought about that a lot, how his father had disciplined his big brain with all its desires and postulations and anxieties to have a purpose: to live for others. This would be meaningful; to work hard to put food on the table and provide for a family. But Bardo couldn't reach the point where this was a need. He thought of Maslow's hierarchy of needs and self-actualization. Could his father have reached that level on his pilgrimages to the beach? The five-mile walk was a long meditation and every time Bardo picked him up at Crab Meadow, his father's face was that of a monk—transcendent. He had conquered anxiety while Bardo was still stuck in the lower levels, concerned mainly with what he discovered when he became a man—the only organ that could effectively distract the big brain.

Perhaps he should have stayed in college to get a master's and then a PhD in psychology to give the brain something to gnaw on. But he was no Freud, despite how he idolized the man. He was more practical, like his father, and he needed money to live the way he wanted to. He knew he neither possessed the drive nor the talent to make a professorship worthwhile. So, he would live a practical life, like his father. Manage a store like his father. But it wasn't enough.

It was a little heartbreaking to see the Grand Prix in front of the gas station with a For Sale sign on its windshield. Bardo walked to the gas station from the Carvel he owned and managed across the street and remembered how his mother always scoffed about the former Mobil station that was now painted red and black: who would want to buy their gas from Hell, she said. Ahmed, the owner, immediately came out of the office when he saw Bardo. He had a smirk on his face, as usual. Ahmed had a big nose, like the noses on the Calabrese side of the family, like Bardo's sister had, but Ahmed's was more hawklike, and he had a bristly black mustache and eyebrows. He always wore a buttoned-down shirt, and slacks that appeared to be stolen from a tux.

"You got a hooker!" Ahmed said.

"I'm sorry?"

"Someone hooked on your car. Wants to take it driving."

"Really."

"Yeah, really. I wrote down the number," Ahmed reached into his pocket. He handed a ripped piece of envelope to Bardo and Bardo looked down at his oily fingers, the phone number with the nines written like g's.

"Did he say he would pay the price?"

"No, he said nothing. If you ask me, he would be a fool."

Bardo scoffed. "It's just a little bit more than the blue book value."

"Too many things wrong. Bald tires. Rusted tailpipe."

A young man came from out of the office and started speaking to Ahmed in what Bardo presumed was Arabic. Ahmed's face changed into one of admiration and gentility when he talked to the young man.

"My son," said Ahmed, when the young man took leave of them. "Heading over to the Middle East Cafe for the happiest hour."

"Oh yeah? I never knew the Middle East had a happy hour."

"There is a waitress there. He likes her. She is Lebanese."

"Oh."

The young man had the blackest hair Bardo had ever seen and he wore designer jeans with a white T-shirt. He must've been in his early twenties and was handsome. The young man waved to his father, put his hands in his pockets and headed toward the restaurant. Bardo put the number in his pocket and told Ahmed he would be back in the morning to leave the car again, hoping that Saturday would be more fruitful. As he pulled out of the driveway, Ahmed's son started slowly jogging toward the restaurant. Bardo caught the light on Larkfield and watched as the young man opened the door flanked by roses growing out of urns at the entrance. Bardo put on his blinker and turned into the parking lot.

The Middle East Cafe was a place he always wanted to visit, and once he asked his mother if she would like to go there for dinner, to try something new, but she resisted (she preferred Fred's Diner where they knew how to make eggplant parmigiana and steak tips). Upon entering, he saw a crowd at the bar and that all of the seats were taken. He immediately felt self-conscious because the surroundings were clearly exotic and foreign—the music, the paintings, the patrons. A young woman approached him; she wore black jeans and a navy-blue ruffled blouse that accentuated her dark features. She was beautiful and young and had elegantly curled black hair and full pink lips. Bardo was virtually speechless when she asked him if he would like a table by the window. After a moment, he gathered himself and followed her. In her wake a wonderful scent wafted about him; it was clean and subtly floral. Bardo presumed this was the girl Ahmed's son fancied.

She sat him at a white-clothed table with a single red rose in a thin glass vase and handed him a menu; Bardo noticed her delicate wrist, the fine bone subtly angled toward the hand, and her white nails. "Can I get you a drink?" she asked.

The business of ordering seemed intimidating with a menu festooned with ribboned letters and English pronunciations too small to read without his glasses. "Budweiser," he said. "I will have a Budweiser."

She looked at his mouth when he answered, and Bardo found that titillating. The waft of blossoms, the curves of her hips, and she was away. Ahmed's son was at the bar with his friends, smoking and laughing and when she passed him, he watched her walk by. Bardo opened the menu, and squinted to read the English pronunciation and descriptions without his glasses.

There were paintings on the walls around him of women in flowing silks and men sitting cross-legged on carpets or lying in the grass in an orchard with animals around them. The people in the paintings all looked like the waitress and Ahmed's son, and they were living exotic lives in a foreign land where nature and sensuality were prominent.

She came back around and placed a bar napkin before him. He felt the subtle warmth of her skin close to his, the warmth below her chin when she bent to place the beer on the table. He noticed she had a silver ring on her pinkie finger. She could not have been any older than seventeen. "Thank you," Bardo said, and she looked at his lips again.

"Will you be eating this evening?" she asked.

Bardo looked down at the menu. "I don't know," he said. "I'm not sure what I would like."

"Do you like meat?"

"Yes, I like meat."

"*Koobideh* is good. Number twenty-six, here," she said, pointing to the menu. Bardo read the description: spicy ground beef mixed with Persian seasonings.

"Okay. I will have that," Bardo said, and handed her his menu. Bardo wanted to say something funny, something to keep her there. His father was good at making conversation, able to make the waitresses laugh; he was always good at extracting the humanity in people and he was liked for it. The long line of people waiting to get into his funeral was proof of this.

Bardo watched the waitress put the order in at the bar. Ahmed's son called her over and they talked. Bardo could hear the music more clearly now, the woman's voice and the soft strumming of a guitar. He wondered about the waitress and Ahmed's son, if they went out. If he touched her. If he was allowed to touch her. Bardo recognized the look on the young man's face and could empathize. He was trying to secure her. She moved away, through a door to the kitchen and the young man turned to his friends, hovering over his drink and cigarette.

Bardo leaned back and noticed the paintings over his table. There were two young lovers speaking with an old man and then in a second painting the old man was sitting with women. Bardo supposed it was his harem. The old man wore a cloak of multi colors; he had a beard. The women all seemed enthralled.

"Lucky guy," Bardo said to himself.

The Middle East became busy with its dinner crowd, and the waitress moved quickly taking orders and filling waters. She put a crystal glass on his table and poured ice water into it, and Bardo thought of the Fountain of Youth in St. Augustine where he visited with his family when he was in junior high; he remembered the dark well, the stone and the woman pouring the life-giving water into a crystal glass "Thank you," he said, barely audibly, and the waitress moved on to the next table. He stared at the man in the paintings, the older man with the gray beard and the turban about his head. When the waitress returned, she placed a porcelain plate in front of him with meat shaped like a phallus, sitting on a bed of yellow rice ornate with jeweled carrots and parsley.

"Can I get you something else," she said, again looking at his mouth.

"No. No thank you." She turned to leave, and he said, "Wait."

The waitress turned around; Bardo imagined putting his hand on the curve of her hip.

"Yes?"

"This man, here in the painting. Who is he? He seems important."

The waitress looked at the paintings. "That is *Sa'dī*. He is an ancient poet."

"I see. And the women in the picture?"

"They are his admirers."

"Right," he said, his big brain jamming. She turned to go and he called out "Wait," again. She turned around, less enthused. He was too old. This was the look on her face: "You're too old." But Bardo persevered. "What does he write about?"

"I don't know. Life?"

"Do you like poetry?

"It's okay."

"Well, what do you like then. What do you do . . . for fun?"

She broke then and smiled a little bit. "I dance."

Bardo smiled. He looked up and noticed that Ahmed's son was staring at them. He seemed to be telepathically beckoning her back. Then he recognized Bardo; Bardo could see the look on his face. He wasn't smiling. He raised his glass to Bardo, and Bardo raised his in return.

There was no doubt that poets had big brains. This is what Bardo thought as he skimmed the poems in a book about Sa'dī that he got from the library. He read the book at night, or tried to, before he fell asleep. There was one poem he thought he almost understood. It was about a dancer:

The Dancer

I heard how, to the beat of some quick tune,
There rose and danced a Damsel like the moon,
Flower-mouthed and Pâri-faced; and all around her
Neck-stretching Lovers gathered close; but, soon

A flickering lamp-flame caught her skirt, and set
Fire to the flying gauze. Fear did beget

Trouble in that light heart! She cried amain.
Quoth one among her worshipers, "Why fret,

Tulip of Love? Th' extinguished fire hath burned
Only one leaf of thee; but I am turned
To ashes—leaf and stalk, and flower and root—
By lamp-flash of thine eyes!"—"Ah, Soul concerned

Solely with self!"—she answered, laughing low,
"If thou wert Lover thou hadst not said so.
Who speaks of the Belov'd's woe is not his
Speaks infidelity, true Lovers know!"

He hadn't admitted to himself that he was going to return to the Middle East Cafe to see the waitress; in fact, he had no plan. He only knew that he had to borrow the book of poems and read some of them. Perhaps he had the idea of going to lunch and discussing poetry with the waitress as a way of getting to know her; he could not say for sure. But he thought about Ahmed's son and the waitress a lot; he wondered during the day, wondered in the evening, and wondered before bed, if they were with each other; if she was letting him do things to her that Bardo wanted to do.

He was almost asleep when the phone rang.
    "Hello?"
    "Hi . . . Bardo?"
    "Yeah."
    "This is Donna!"
    "Oh, Donna, hey, how've you been."
    "Hangin' in there, you know how it is. And you?"
    "Uh, busy. Very busy."
    "I hear ya. You moved, huh. Your mother gave me your new number."
    "Yeah, found a small house off Larkfield. Tired of paying rent."
    "Wow, a house, Bardo. You must be doing very well for yourself. You still at the Carvel?"
    "Yup."

"You've been there a long time, huh. Ten years?"

"Something like that."

"Good for you. How's your mother doing? We didn't talk much when I called."

"She's okay."

"I bet she misses your father, huh."

"Uhh, yeah. Of course."

"You know the reason I'm calling is that I found your electric razor. I thought maybe you'd like to have it back."

"My razor? Oh."

"It was in my suitcase, from when we went to Florida!"

"Huh. Well, I bought a new one, so you can keep it, I guess."

"That's ridiculous! Return the one you bought and I'll give you this one. They're expensive."

"It's okay. Really."

"Well listen, I was thinking, you know, it's been so long since we've seen each other. Let's go out and have a drink. We used to have so much fun! And I can give you back the razor. What do you think? Are you seeing anyone?"

"No. No not right now."

"The guy I'm dating is sweet. Wants to get serious."

"Really! Good!"

"Yes. And he's Jewish!"

"Does your mother like him?"

"Yeah, she likes him. My mother liked you too, Bardo, even though you're not Jewish. Anyway, this guy, well, he's cute. But," Donna sighed audibly through the phone. "You know what I mean."

"Maybe," Bardo said.

"How about Saturday night. One drink."

"Um. Well..."

"Oh come on, Bardo, don't make me beg."

"Okay. Sure. Yeah why not."

Donna was dressed to kill. She wore a low-cut sweater and a short leather skirt with daggers for heels. When Bardo kissed her left cheek and smelled the vodka on her breath, he knew it was going to be a long night. They met at Coco's outside tiki bar where the older crowd congregated amidst a fake thatched roof, kerosene torches, and potted palm plants. The pink sunset over the harbor of boats gently rocking in the deep green seawater made the place more palatable than other bars where they played rap music so loud it intruded upon every thought, and the younger generation danced their esoteric dances, which seemed more like posing and fighting than dancing. Here, the women had boob jobs and the men, hair transplants, and everyone was divorced, but it was outside in the fresh air and Bardo liked to scope out the boats in hopes of finding one he could afford with the money from the sale of the car.

They made it through a round of pleasantries and ordered dinner, and Bardo drank more than he wanted to nullify the situation of eating dinner with an ex, who clearly had ideas about where the night was headed. Then they danced. That was the one thing they both loved to do, dance, and they did it well together. Bardo knew to drink just enough to improve his body's fluidity, but not too much that he got sloppy. Donna could hold her drink well, and she knew how to move her body to the music, having taken dance lessons for years. Also, she had a tight little dancer body, that Bardo liked to watch do its thing. After about midnight, the dancers danced and the drinkers got drunk, and the music made it possible to be in the body, but leave the mind behind.

Bardo knew Donna shouldn't drive home, so they got in his car and he drove her to the house she shared with her mother.

"Your mother's not working tomorrow, right? She can take you back to Coco's to get the car." Donna stared blankly at the front door, highlighted from the headlights of the Grand Prix. She was frustrated, aware that he was making her decisions for her.

"I forgot to give you the razor, she said. "It's in my car. We can go back and get it."

"No. That isn't necessary."

They sat in silence and darkness staring at the illuminated door.

"You should go in," Bardo said. "It's late."

"No," she said. "Shut the car off. I want to sit here a little bit longer."

Bardo shut off the car and the lights and opened the windows to sober up. "So what's this guy's name? You never told me his name."

"Morty. Mordecai. It's an angel's name; at least to me it is." Donna shifted in her seat, continued to stare at the place where the door was. "And I beckoned him and he came to me," she said. "I never told anyone."

"You beckoned him? How?"

"After you and I broke up last year, I wrote down all the things I wanted in a man. I rolled up the piece of paper and stuck it in one of those cheap wine bottles with the twist off caps and drove to Crab Meadow in the rain. It's such a lonely place in the rain, Bardo. It is just so god-awful lonely there with the gulls crying and the wind blowing and no one around for miles and the water was just so goddamn gray—. I threw the bottle into the water, and it was rough, and the bottle just disappeared and I couldn't see it anymore. I came back the next day to check if it washed ashore, but it didn't and I thought to myself, *Good. It's out there.* And then a few months later, I met Morty through Jewish Date, and he's everything that was in that bottle."

"That's great!" Bardo said, thrilled he was off the hook.

"But now I'm scared, because I feel—cornered. Cornered by my own life. Do you know what I mean? I know you know what I mean, Bardo. I know you know."

"But I think it's different for you, Donna. Because you'll get over it. You will. You'll see past it. You're just afraid now, but the fear will pass."

"He wants to have kids. Buy a house for us. He's looking. It's happening, just happening on its own, and I don't have to do anything about it. I don't have to work at it."

"That's good. Isn't it?"

"But you know, I need to let loose sometimes. I'm gonna need that. Like when we got high and went skinny dipping after my cousin Louise's wedding. That was so crazy and fun. Wasn't it?"

"It was. But you can do that with Morty. Mordecai."

"Mordecai doesn't smoke. He's really straight-laced. But he'll be a great dad." Donna leaned on the car door with her elbow and propped up her head on her hand. She spied Bardo through the corners of her eyes. Bardo remembered that he had a picture of her doing this, and how alluring she looked. "But then there's you," she said. Donna leaned over and put her hand on his shorts and started to massage his inner thigh. With her touch, blood rushed like a river. Bardo closed his eyes and thought of the waitress and Ahmed's son. He thought of her touching him. He wondered what it would be like to feel her touch, her forbidden, soft, tentative touch. Donna started to unzip his shorts. He caught her hand. Outside there was a sound of crickets; his father once told him that was the sign the summer was over, the end of something.

"Donna," he said. "Go inside."

She drunkenly shook her head. "No."

"Yes. Because I don't love you and Morty does. So go inside."

She thumped back in her seat. Bardo could feel her looking at him in the darkness; he remembered the intensity of her eyes, the tears, the way she nearly hyperventilated when he told her he didn't want to see her anymore. He was afraid it could happen again, now. Then a light went on in the house and Donna looked up. She let out a long sigh. "I'm tired," she said, "I'm so tired and you're just such a bastard." She grabbed her purse, opened the door, and got out of the car.

On Sunday, Bardo took a long walk to Crab Meadow when it looked like rain, because he thought he should know the loneliest place on Earth. It started out as a mist and then a warm rain, soft and delicate on his face and he walked in the company of his own thoughts and the swish of the cars on the road. He reached the Sound with its detritus of sunny days—a Coke can, a plastic shovel, a flip flop, wrappers to popsicles—and he walked and walked aside the steely gray water and its warm froth and the mournful sound of the gulls. And he thought of Donna's bottle, somewhere out there bobbing in the waves, and he thought of his father's grave, with the dirt now patted down from his mother's footsteps and the dirt now being engulfed by the green grass, and he thought of Regina, and her *Feminist's Response to Freud*, and how she preferred Jung over Freud, because, according to her, the anima that Jung realized was really the forsaken feminine deity coming through; and he thought of Freud who believed art and spirituality stemmed from the suppressed sexuality of mankind, and how Jung disagreed wholeheartedly with this and believed that these were entities of the soul, and how Freud fainted in the presence of Jung when he broached the topic of the peat bog corpses because he thought Jung wanted him dead, and he thought again of Regina who paraphrased Jung when she said that for Freud, in all his irreligiosity, the penis was the daimon that replaced Yahweh and was just as demanding.

Bardo took off his soiled sneakers and let the froth curl about his toes and he thought he might like to be that bottle bobbing somewhere on the other side of the Earth heading to who knows where; this was not a death wish, to submerge himself in the gray water and let it take him, not a death wish, but the desire to be found somewhere else.

Bardo thought about how his mother once told him that his father had wanted to become a police officer after he came home from the war. But by the time he got back to the states, Florence was already 28 years old, and he knew if he wanted to have a life with her, he had to marry her immediately and provide for her and the family they wanted. Hearing this disappointed Bardo, he wanted his father to possess the wherewithal and shrewdness needed for self-fulfillment. And yet, there were the walks to the Sound to this very place. Bardo would drive here on Sunday afternoons to find his old man sitting on one of the benches softly whistling, looking up at the gulls or out toward the horizon, his arms stretched out across the bench, opening himself up to the world around him. If Crab Meadow in the rain was the loneliest place to Donna, Crab Meadow in the sunshine was a place of pure bliss to his father, who had walked his many miles to get to it.

Bardo headed home and the clouds started to part. To the west, the sun and some patches of blue were apparent by the time he reached Larkfield Road. When he approached the Middle East Café, there was a CLOSED sign on the door, and yet the parking lot was filled with cars. He could hear music and the shaking of a tambourine. Bardo was certain Ahmed's son was in there, because he was one of them, and his heart panged. For the hell of it, Bardo went to the door and pulled the handle, but it was locked. Then he heard cheering and the music got louder. He walked around back to where there was a parting of the curtains. He peered in, closer, and saw her above him, all shimmer and veils, dancing to the tambourine, to the drum, to the music in his heart.

CHAPTER 6
PANIC
NICOLETTA

It was a fine autumn day and the trees and vines in back of the dunes were illuminated in gold and vermillion leaves. I walked farther than I ever had before, farther than Robert and I had walked, to the sand cliffs and beyond. They weren't ominous at all, and in the light, they were something spectacular—broad cliffs of sand that reached upwards of 100 feet—and beyond them a sandbar where the currents spilled gentle waves. There were downed trees, marsh grass, driftwood. I was filled with a sense of freedom and adventure being in this place, like the time, as a child, I rode my bike past the entrance to my street, to a horse farm and beyond to where there was a small orchard of cherry trees. I parked my bike and climbed the trees to eat the cherries and they were wonderfully sweet, and I ate so many, my hands were stained in juice. The sand bar where the sea sprawled gently and where slender white birds stopped to fish, gave me this same sense of awe of all that was out there worth exploring and my spirit, so dormant and repressed from fear, leapt at it with hunger and joy.

The reality of this was that I did not actually walk the beach to the sand cliffs: this was a vision during a meditation session in Sabine's store.

The shades were closed, and we sat on old couch cushions in front of the fountain. This was our fourth session, and still there was nothing about Robert's fiancé, Elena, but there was something changing—a shift, Sabine called it. I started to like the sessions; I looked forward to sitting quietly, listening to the flowing water and the chimes hanging outside the shop. Sabine put the chimes there purposely for me, because when she asked me what particular sound relaxed me, I said chimes. It was the chimes that centered me and allowed me to feel comfortable in my body.

Sabine sat on the pillow in front of me with her legs crossed. Her hair was not tidily pinned up, as she wore it for a day in the store receiving customers; it was down, loose and coarse around her shoulders. She wore a Rangers T-shirt and jeans with an afghan blanket around her legs. I had one as well, to counteract the drafts.

The door of the shop suddenly opened and Esmerelda appeared, carrying a stack of books. She seemed more mature, with her hair down and not in braids, and in the way she carried herself, she was less childlike and more composed.

"I see that you were successful," Sabine said, as Esmerelda walked past her, toward the back of the store. "Esmerelda is writing a report on Eleanor Roosevelt."

Esmerelda stopped and gave out a big sigh. "This should at least get me started."

"Sounds very interesting," I said.

Esmerelda glanced at her mother. "I'm going to go make my outline."

"Good luck," Sabine said. "There is soup on the stove for dinner. It just needs to be heated."

Esmerelda nodded her head and just as she shut the back door to the apartment they lived in over the store, I heard an internal voice. It said, *she is his*. We went back to meditating and I tried to focus on the chimes, but the voice came back even louder. *His. She is his.*

"She is his," I said aloud. "It just came to me—a message."

Sabine started to say something and then stopped herself. She knew exactly what those words meant.

"Christophe is Esmerelda's father."

"*Father* Christophe?"

"Yes."

We sat for a moment in silence, and my brain spun with all that was implied.

"But you were so young..."

"When I first met him, yes. But we were reunited later. It was a time in my life when I was looking for answers, much like you are now. I had a fiancé, but I did not want to marry him. There was a retreat house that the people in my church often went to, and I decided to go for a month after I graduated university. Christophe was there. I had always suspected something—my feelings about him. And then it became very obvious, to me, how I felt about him: I was in love with him. I was embarrassed and ashamed to be thinking of a priest in this way. But at the retreat house, it was a separate place; there was nothing outwardly religious about it. It was instead, remarkably romantic, with its ocean views and stone walls and gardens. And it was here that we discovered something new between us. Instead of priest and pupil, we were...woman and man."

"Geez, what is it about psychics and priests."

"Priests live internal lives. They commune directly with God, while we interpret His messages."

At this point I had not confided in Sabine my hidden feelings for Robert, that I was attracted to him, as she was attracted to Christophe. So, this revelation was somewhat uncanny, and on some level, a possible warning that no *Thorn Birds* relationship could survive. But on another level, there was intrigue and desire to see this thing through, to take it as far as I could, to discover what I could about the woman and man part of our relationship, just as she had.

"What's important is that I can make a living here and I can give our child an uncomplicated life," she said. "I cannot deny that sometimes I want to go back, because I miss my home. I miss the food and the language and the love that I know to be there. But this place—this place with its stark winters and snow and ice—this too is mine. I have even become a hockey fan," she said, gesturing to her shirt.

"I would have never pictured you as a hockey fan," I said.

"There are surprises everywhere," Sabine said. "Contradictions. Like, for instance, your nose."

I burst out laughing. "My nose?"

"You have told me more than once that it makes you self-conscious, because you think of it as a flaw. But to me, it is an emblem of strength. It is a good, strong nose, and maybe someday you will see it that way."

"Probably not," I said.

Instead of deterring me from pursuing Robert in a romantic way, I was even more obsessed about seeing him again. After weeks of not hearing from him, I decided to visit him in the rectory to put an end to the mystery. I parked on the street, near the school, a considerable distance away from my mother's house so she wouldn't see my car if she walked by. I sat in the car, mulling over the things I should say, and how I should say them, but could not focus on a plan. It was time to stop thinking and just act, so I forced myself out of the car.

I went to the rectory door and knocked. Inside the foyer a light was on and there was an open book on a table. On the wall above the table was a painting of the Virgin Mary in an emerald-green robe reading a book while being visited by an angel. The angel appeared over her shoulder and looked like a woman; she carried a staff, and had multi-colored wings. As I was engrossed in the painting, a man appeared in the doorway suddenly. It was Father Crane, one of the priests who had been there since my confirmation; the last time I saw him, he came to give my father his last rites. He was older now, and I doubt he recognized me, nonetheless, I still felt self-conscious, like I was doing something wrong by intruding on their sanctity. I could feel my heart pumping blood to my veins, and I dug my fingernails of one hand in to the palm of the other to distract myself from my anxiety. "Hello Father," I said. "I am looking for Father Kirton. Is he here?"

"Oh yes, yes. I believe he is in his room. Come in, won't you?"

I crossed the threshold and felt it immediately—the aura of the place: it was a stillness that comes from the passage of time, of spiritual lives lived but now somewhere else. Father Crane closed the door. I stopped to gaze at the painting and Father Crane noticed me. "Ah yes," he said. "One of the many paintings of the Annunciation. That is the angel Gabriel there and that is the Blessed Mother. Well, Mary, I mean, before she was a mother."

"It is lovely," I said.

"Indeed. One of my favorites. You can really get the sense that the angel Gabriel sprung upon her, and she had no idea what was coming. From then on, her life as she knew it, was over. See here, she is reading," he said pointing to the open book. "Can you imagine being visited by an angel of God while you're absorbed in a book? And yet, it was the greatest moment of hope for all the world."

Mary's countenance didn't appear shocked or horrified. It was demure and shy, docile, as she always seemed, as men had painted her again and again, throughout history.

"Come, follow me. Let's see if Father Kirton is available." We walked down the hall and Father Crane knocked at a door. I looked down at the perfectly straight lines of the marble tile, the same marble tile I focused on while walking the line up to communion, weak in the knees, terrified of making a mistake, dropping the eucharist, accidentally stepping on it or tripping into the priest. Every Sunday, the same thing, the terror of being made to walk to the altar, as if I were to be sacrificed instead of being given a flat, stale wafer.

"Father? Father are you in there? There is a young woman to see you here."

Robert opened the door; he was dressed in his habit and wore glasses. When he looked at me, I could see the horror in his eyes. I wanted to run away; this was a bad idea, and I should've waited for him to contact me.

"Oh hello, Nicoletta, so nice of you to come. Father, this is Florence Russo's daughter."

"I thought you looked familiar!"

We reminisced a bit about my confirmation year and then Father Crane left us.

"Care to go for a walk?" Robert asked.

"Yes, sure."

"I will get my coat."

I peered into his room. It was sexless, with a twin bed, shelves of books, a rocking chair, and lamp. Robert grabbed his coat from the closet and we walked out, toward the schoolyard in back of the church. Dusk was falling fast, and the last of the leaves were falling from the trees; we swished through them as we walked, and I thought of walking to school through leaves just like these and them sticking to my shoes by the dew that drenched them in early morning. We walked the edge of the playground where my father used to take us when we were young, where I ran and played during recess, where I smoked cigarettes in the shadows of the trees, and sipped from stolen bottles of wine.

"I'm sorry I disturbed you," I said. "I know I should've called. That would've been the right thing to do."

"It's okay," he said. "Yes, you caught me by surprise, but I welcome the company."

I took a breath, stopped walking and then it poured out of me, a confession: "It's not working. I have to tell you that it's not working. I tried to find answers. I tried meditation and nothing is coming. I don't really think I am a clairvoyant; I am just a lonely woman. A terribly lonely and bored woman whose mind gets the best of her. I thought it best to come here and tell you this, so you wouldn't continue to have false hopes."

He stopped, looked at me and smiled, "You are an absolute breath of fresh air with how honest you are with yourself and other people. I'm sorry you're lonely," he said. "I know what it is to be lonely."

"So, it that all we are? Two lonely people who had a moment?"

He looked away, at the sky with fading streaks of color, the darkened trees. The train horn blew for the five o'clock; people were going home to their families. I thought of Thomas, I was late to go pick him up from daycare. I could feel the anxiety of the situation in my body, the vibrations in my nerves, how I was desperately trying to fit something into my life that didn't belong.

"No," he said. "That is not all we are."

He looked at me intently; it was an invitation, and I went toward him, but my heel got stuck in the grass, and I lost my balance. He grabbed my elbow and he was closer now, and I was inside the place where he held himself, where he experienced his loneliness, and I found a warmth there, his hands, warm. But the engine of panic was too much to be eradicated; I felt it, all the anxiety that I shoved into a tight corner inside myself to act normal, to get myself here; it shot up to the surface like a geyser. My throat constricted; I was going to hyperventilate. This was not something he was supposed to see.

"Nicky, are you okay?"

And that's when I saw her face, just underneath the surface of the water, white, the eyes open, white, the mouth open, the arms spread wide, the body half in light, half descending, drifting.

"She drowned!" I yelled, breathlessly. "I can see her face in the water! She drowned!"

There was darkness all around now and the lights suddenly went on outside the school.

"Take deep breaths," he said, "Easy."

He held both my hands now, to settle me, and I watched his lips, trying to make sense of what he was saying. "Look at me, Nicky. Breathe with me. In for three out for six," and I did what he told me to do and I breathed. The panic started to subside, and I was drenched in a cold sweat and exhausted. He walked me to my car, and I fumbled for my keys in my purse. I was disoriented.

"They found her car on one side of the lake and her body on the other," he said. "They ruled it an accident, but I've always wondered, what if it wasn't? Why would she go to the lake without me? She had a fear of water: it didn't make sense. They said there were some bruises on her legs, like she had a fall. But nothing was conclusive. So, I've had to grapple with the mystery—of whether she took her own life. And why. This is what I want to know."

I put the key in the lock of the door. I opened it. I had to get to Thomas; I was late. This was the thought in my head: I was late and this was all too much for me.

CHAPTER 7

THE VIRGIN

ROBERT KIRTON

He had to admit to himself that the idea of Elena was dissolving, while the tangibility, the temptation of Nicoletta was becoming more apparent. He was well aware that this was a means out, an exit door, away from suffering and into a new way of being. But it had all the characteristics of a classic temptation. It was clear that Nicoletta was vulnerable as he was vulnerable, but he insisted that vulnerability was no reason to start a relationship of any kind. He had to keep in mind his role as a model citizen, that others were watching and there were expectations from someone in his position. Besides, the focus had to be on the suffering, according to everything he had learned as a priest. You can't take the easy way out. Mental and physical suffering was the "medium of God's choicest mercies." He had to stick with it, abide in Christ, and see where it could take him spiritually. This is what he told himself day in and day out.

This was the theological way of seeing things. The reality of the issue was that he was depressed and that depression was insignificant when he was with Nicoletta. It was her warmth; it was her unabashed acknowledgement of her own flaws; it was her way of being human.

While others tried so desperately to hide their shortcomings or pretended not to see them, she bore them. She did not try to eradicate them, like Elena did.

His feelings toward Nicoletta were compounded by the fact that his interactions with the parishioners had become stale. Even the writing of his homilies, which he had once enjoyed, were driven by a template that seemed to have lost its potency. He kept a journal to store his personal anecdotes and feelings. From there he wove scriptures into his message, connecting the old with the modern by relating these to parishioner's daily lives. Write, research, relate. And during this process, something opened, a wellspring of thought, of feeling, of knowing exactly what to say, and how to say it. He only had to sit down and get to work to make it happen. Was it the Holy Spirit guiding him or the fact that he had always been a good writer? He didn't know. But lately the wellspring seems to have dried up. His thoughts were fragmented and discontinuous; the whole thing was forced, like he was trying to find a path through the wood that had been grown over.

Although his homilies had been crafted and impactful on paper, he was never comfortable delivering them. He could never live up to the rock star priests who had the parishioners swooning or laughing; he wasn't an actor and he wasn't confident enough to put on a show. He could not separate himself from the reactions of the audience; he was acutely aware of their boredom, how they checked their watches, yawned incessantly, or stared blankly at the pew in front of them, and this made him lose the thread of his speech, trip over his words, or go off on a tangent. It was then that he felt like an imposter, that he didn't have what it took to reach people. Similarly, at the more celebratory sacraments, weddings, baptisms, communions and confirmations, he was awkward as the figurehead of the ceremony and it rattled him.

It was in the intimate setting of the sacrament of confession that he felt he could properly do his work. He knew deeply what it was to be a flawed human being, insecure, struggling to fit into the world. In the booth, he kept empathy at the center of the conversation, and this put people at ease. He knew it by the distinct switch in mood, from a tone of despondency to one of faith; he was their guide, their counselor regarding ideas they might find fruitful and new ways of interpreting old problems. It was a compassionate act: a spiritual food by which he fed himself and the main reason he continued to be a priest.

He especially enjoyed the weekday masses in the chapel with the older parishioners who were there in earnest. Father Stransky usually said the mass, here, because it was silent, without the choir, and simplified; he was near retirement and no longer wished to be a part of the weekend family masses. Father Stransky walked very slowly and breathed very heavily, and he often coughed loudly during the service and this disturbed the placidity of it. When he did not serve, he sat in the back pew and stayed for a long time afterward, listening to the baptism fountain behind the altar. Robert saw that he liked to pray and then nod off to sleep there, in the morning, with the light coming through the stained glass, as it sprinkled color across his old folded hands.

The intimate setting of the chapel, the illumination of St. Anthony's lilies behind the small altar, the ritual of breaking bread with others—communion—this is where he felt the presence of God. The mass had always been a source of comfort to him, a place he could escape to from the dysfunction of his home life, his father and the booze and the impetuous assaults on the family. Mass was a kind of shelter where he and his mother went to find solace. It was a place where he saw the imploring faces of others, eyes closed, hands clasped, lips moving, and he felt a kinship with them. He had always struggled with talking to God, but it was here that he felt as if he didn't have to, he was immersed in people talking to God and this in itself was his prayer—a living prayer—as well.

Father Gregory always sat next to him during the morning masses in the chapel. He was younger than Kirton, was raised on a farm in Kansas; Gregory was gentle and soft-spoken and had hands like a woman; this was one of the first things Robert noticed about him—his delicate female hands with long slender fingers and ivory-white nails. His chin was always smooth with no indication of facial hair, his eyes a pale green, like the color of the sky before a summer storm. He sometimes knocked at Robert's door at night, when his light was on, to discuss theology. But sometimes it was late, and there would be the knock and Robert would open the door and the young man would not say a word, only stand there, waiting for Robert to acknowledge his evident distress. He would offer him a cup of herbal tea, and the two would sit at Robert's small table and look out at the statue of the Virgin, with the spotlight at her feet, making her appear like an apparition in the night.

One night, when Gregory sat across from Robert at the table, he seemed smaller; he stared at Robert like a woman would, wanting to be held. Gregory looked at the floor. He pulled up his left knee and supported it with his hands. Robert remembered the protocol of setting a tone of calmness and safety. He had known for some time that Gregory was struggling with something, but the young priest had yet to confide in his friend. Sitting across from Gregory, Robert was too weary for such a conversation; he welcomed Gregory out of a sense of duty, and because he did not know how to set his boundaries. Being an empath, he strove to help everyone he could, even if it was at his own expense. Robert waited for Gregory to speak. He had that feeling he would get just before a confession begins, the feeling of curiosity, but more so, apprehension. He thought back to a woman, years ago, a young English woman who had confessed to having the desire to kill her baby. As a young priest, inexperienced, he was shocked and visibly overcome by his own emotional response. Every confession reminded him of that one; there was always the fear that it would be something he could not handle.

Gregory released his knee, brought the cup to his lips, but the tea was too hot, so he set it back down. The old table rocked a little as he set the cup down on his saucer.

"Tell me about your vocation. How did it happen?" he asked Robert.

Robert paused, touched the handle of his own cup; it felt smooth and warm. "It was vague," he said, becoming a bit uncomfortable, but wanting to tell the truth.

Gregory uncrossed his legs then crossed them again. "What do you mean, 'vague'?"

"I mean, I'm not sure if it was there at all." Robert leaned back in his chair, smoothed the table top with his index finger. "I'm struggling with this now."

Gregory's face lightened. He was not the only one with an internal conflict.

"I often think of what Augustine said, how the disorder of the soul is its own punishment. Is every punishment a means of purification?"

The smoke from the cup was becoming faint; they were going to play this game again of talking about things without really talking about them.

"I'm not sure 'purification' is the appropriate term," Robert said. "The journey of suffering, the struggle, eventually leads to acceptance, and then transformation, if the person abides with it, and that is something to live for. It is this way for the irreligious as well."

It was a simplified response, something someone might say at an AA meeting.

"Yes, of course," Gregory said. "If one abides with it, it starts to lose its potency. The garden grows up around the weeds. But I don't want to apologize for my life anymore. Not to myself, not to others. Not to God. But every day, I wake up feeling ashamed, wanting to be different, seeking forgiveness for things I haven't yet done. The shame has a life of its own. I want to learn to let it go. I want to let it go."

Gregory took the cup with its saucer in his hands. He took a sip, placed the cup and saucer back down. There was something about the movement that proved conviction. Robert felt at ease now; the focus was off him.

"What are you ashamed of, Gregory?" he asked.

Gregory shifted in his seat, stared down at the table, at the cups of tea, at Robert's hand in proximity to his cup. He moved his right hand and placed it over Robert's and gently slid his thumb over Robert's knuckles. A pulse of heat went down Robert's neck and into his shoulders. His face flushed. He pulled his hand away and placed it in his lap.

Gregory looked down at the floor. "I thought it might be very obvious to you what I struggle with."

Robert looked at the young man before him and felt like a fool. He had been so preoccupied with his own struggle that he didn't see what was right in front of him.

"I guess I was wrong. I'm sorry." Gregory said, and then sat up straight. "But maybe you didn't want to see it, because it would be a problem you would need to confront."

"Forgive me," Robert said. "I—"

Gregory drew in a long breath, let it out, and interrupted Robert. "I had a dream I was walking through a crowd of people in New York City. You know what it's like to walk in a crowd in New York, right? No one looks at one another. Everyone seems as if they are shut off inside, moving through space just to get to somewhere else. Well, I too was one of these people and then I saw him—Christ. He was staring at me from across the street. The people were moving about him, like they didn't know who he was. But I knew who he was and he knew who I was. The look in his eyes—it's hard to describe it. It's not like what you see in the paintings or the statues: it wasn't mournful or reflective or self-assured. He had the same look a teacher has before he calls on you in class because you know the answer. That's what I saw when I moved toward him. And then I woke up." Gregory straightened in his chair and looked at Robert. "But do you know that sometimes I think maybe I've gotten it wrong. That it wasn't a vocation at all; he wasn't looking at me like I had something to share with others, like I was to be his pupil doing his work. He was looking at me because he wanted to see how I would handle what he had laced my spirit with, how I would get myself out of the snafu that was my life. And I thought—I thought that maybe you were struggling with the same thing. These late-night talks—"

"No," Robert said sharply. "I mean, that is not what I am struggling with."

Gregory stared at Robert and recognition flashed across his face. He stood up. "I'm sorry," he said and made a motion to leave. Robert caught him by the wrist.

"But I am no different than you in that I suffer too. With who I am. And what I need. And there was no vocation. There was no directive. There was only the need for a safe haven." Robert let go of Gregory's wrist. "Don't leave like this. I am sorry too. I am sorry that maybe, that, I hurt you."

"What is it, then? What could it be? Is it love?"

He wanted to tell Gregory, Yes. Yes, it was love. The woman I loved may have loved God more than she loved me. This is what he wanted to say. So, it was love, and the love, the triangle, between him and the woman he loved and God was complicated. But instead, he said: "Yes. Yes. It is a love that haunts me every day of my life and like you, I feel as if God is fooling with me and I am about to crack, because I have outgrown this life—this safe, predictable, solitary life, and I don't know what to do."

Gregory sat back down. He gazed at the illuminated Virgin on the lawn. "Well, we're just two peas in a pod, now aren't we."

Robert sighed. He had felt a weight lift with the confession. "I'm sorry if I've hurt you in any way."

Gregory bravely looked at Robert and smiled sadly. "It is getting late. I should be going."

Robert nodded his head.

Gregory sipped the rest of his tea. He stood up again. "I'll pray for you, Father," he said, and left.

Mount Paul was a novitiate for the Paulist Fathers up a small mountain in northern New Jersey where he grew up. He and his mother went every Sunday in the family Oldsmobile with rust eating at the door edges and tire wells. Robert remembered the long driveway through the woods, the small stones popping out from under the Oldsmobile's tires, the starkness of the bare, wooded world in winter, the verdant life of the trees in deep summer. The little amount of heat coming from the nearly defunct heater was never enough to kill the February chill; with the air conditioning eternally broken, the windows were always down in summer to let in blasts of humid air.

The novitiate overlooked a lake that was flanked by rock boulders on one side, a marsh on the other, and a dock and small beach at the end of a path from the main building. Robert walked the footpath around the lake often; he would bring a book and a sandwich and spend the afternoon on the top of the granite cliff that marked the northern part of the lake, listening to the birdsong. In the summer, he would swim, especially in the morning, in the deep water that was the epitome of stillness and silence that brought a freshness to his mind and spirit. It was a place of rejuvenation, a refuge when his irascible father would pick on him and his brothers or chastise his mother for not doing some task just as he liked. But on Sundays, the focal point was the chapel, the stained-glass windows forming no deity or spiritual scene, just a simple collage of colored light. Above a simple altar was the risen Christ, detached from the backdrop of a metal cross, his arms spread wide to embrace all who sought him. Robert often looked up at the chest, fully exposed aside his draped robe, and saw a lamb's face there. Even as an adolescent he had made the connection; he recalled the studies of the Iliad and the Odyssey and how the Greeks had slaughtered animals to purify themselves. Christ walked into his own slaughter to purify the world.

There were a few other families who worshipped at Mount Paul along with the novitiates, and Elena's family was one of them. He had known her as a child; she was in his second-grade class, a quiet girl who always wore her hair in a tight bun, simple dresses, stockings, and shiny black patent leather shoes. She went to Catholic school in the next town after that year, and then he didn't see her again until she was in high school and her family started attending Mount Paul masses. She would come to mass fashionable dressed in a skirt and a pressed, collared shirt, always with stockings, always with leather pumps that matched her outfit. She was elegant and sophisticated; her parents were first generation Italians from Florence and they carried themselves with dignity and instilled this in their daughter.

Robert did his best to be inconspicuous about his feelings, but he found it difficult to not stare at her at church. Sometimes she would catch him staring and then look down, becoming flushed in the face. His mother noticed this and cautioned him to not get his hopes up; a girl like that often dates young men with money. But Robert was smitten and determined and on a Holy Thursday seder the Paulists gave to have the community sit and celebrate the Last Supper with them, Robert and Elena were given the task of making Elena's mother's chocolate cream pie from scratch. Elena was very serious about the task, and had her mother's recipe carefully written out on an index card in a neat and perfectly legible handwriting; she insisted on abiding by every measurement exactly, using dry measuring cups for the dry ingredients and a wet measuring cup for the cream, and a double boiler for the chocolate, which she had brought from her mother's kitchen. He tried to make her laugh, tease her about her perfectionism, but he couldn't help but feel a little intimidated by the severity in with she approached the task and her insistence in getting things right.

While the pie cooled, he took her for a walk along the lake on the footpath and pointed out the different birds that were flittering in the trees. The trees were just beginning to bud and the crocuses were up; he picked her one to put in her bun. He observed her, the way she impeccably balanced herself while walking over rocks, the way her body looked in straight-legged jeans, her French-manicured nails, the pink petal color on her lips, her dark eyes. After a while of walking and talking, he could see that she was feeling more relaxed. She had told him that ballet was everything to her, that she mostly ate salad, tuna fish, and crackers, and denied herself much of the world's pleasures to curb her mind and body for the rigors of dance. She told him that when she dances, it's all worth it; it's a kind of virtuousness, a freedom from the tainted world at large. She confessed that if she didn't pursue dance, she would become a nun, because the religious life and keeping a vow to God fascinated her. Robert had never met anyone like her; most girls he knew were abstract to him, interested in what others were doing, what others were wearing, and whom others were dating. He had never met anyone like himself, harboring a secret curiosity about the religious life.

The first time he saw her dance— she was the snow queen in the Nutcracker—he witnessed the real creature that lived inside the anxious young woman. This creature was confident and playful and sensual. He could not sleep that night, electrified with desire for this other Elena. He had played it safe for over a year, not wanting to frighten her away with his need to be close to her. Also, it was not the right time: he had just started college and Elena had just won a scholarship for ballet. He continued to cultivate the friendship from afar, writing to her about his classes and burgeoning philosophies. She wrote to him about her strict routines and work ethic and the politics and egos of the world of dance in Manhattan. He worried about her incessantly, being in the city alone, and called her when he could, between exams and on breaks. He gathered from what she told him that she led a fairly secluded life, did not have many friends, and he worried about that, but also felt secure in that he was her only confidante.

It was one summer, years later, when they were both home that they walked the path around the lake after mass and she asked him to marry her. From her letters, he knew that disillusionment had set in—she was no longer enchanted with the dream of becoming a principal ballerina. She was passed up for the role of Odette in Swan Lake; she had become a ballerina typecast for only secondary roles. This is what she told him and he couldn't help but wonder if this was accurate or just her overly severe interpretation of the situation. He was applying for grad school at the time and had written to her less often. He had met other young women in college and slept with them, and although he did not fall in love with any of them, some great itch was finally soothed.

They went for a bike ride one August morning on the path around the lake, and the water was glistening in the late summer sunlight and the trees were heavy with dark green foliage, the kind that had reached the end of their growth and can do nothing else but transform in color and then drop off and die. The clouds crowded the sun surreptitiously and soon it began to rain hard. "Oh! Oh my Gosh!" he heard Elena calling behind him and then laughing. "Who would've thought?" Robert veered off the trail toward a refuge he knew in the woods, a small cabin that the elder priests used to study and pray in solitude. They parked their bikes and ran to the front porch as the rain splashed down hard on the roof, cascading off it in waterfalls at the corners and rushing down the path like a river. They peered in through the window to an old pot belly stove, a neatly made bed, a wooden desk with a chair.

"Let's try the door. Maybe there are towels inside," Robert said, feeling that this was a long shot, because he had come many times before and the door was locked. But this time the door was open, and Robert and Elena entered quietly and slowly, expecting to see someone else who had come in from the rain. "Hello?" Robert called out. "Is anyone here?"

The cabin had a musty, sweet smell, like incense. Its two rooms, a bedroom with a kitchenette and small bathroom were kept tidy, the bed made, the bathroom clean with no indication of use. In a closet off the bathroom were clean towels and he fetched one. Elena walked around the place, reading the different books on the shelves, books written by popes, poets, and saints; a copy of *Alice in Wonderland, a Norton Critical Edition*.

"What a wonderful little place," she said.

The rain came down harder on the roof, and they both looked up toward the rafters, spanned with spider webs and speckled intermittently with nails. He noticed then, as she stood there in the room with him that she was thinner, her wet T-shirt outlining her collar bones and ribs. Elena lay on the bed and closed her eyes. "I can rest here," she said. "I feel like I can rest here."

Robert sat on the bed next to her, noticing a moth wing tangled in a thread hanging from the lamp. He handed her the towel, "You can dry off first," he said.

"It doesn't matter," she said and closed her eyes. He wiped his face and arms, the towel feeling coarse against his skin, as if it were allowed to dry in the open air. He draped the towel over the chair and she grabbed his hand. It was an unexpected move, bold, and a bit reckless. "Will you marry me?" she asked.

The sunlight poured in through the window as he removed her wet clothes; it was here that he realized how fragile she really was. She had pared-down muscle and bone where breasts should've been, breasts only indicated by pale pink nipples, like petals on either side of the meridian of her body. She bore his gentle thrusts and maneuverings, willing her body to submit. Although he was aroused by her nymph-like body, he wondered at the translucency of her skin, he could see the workings going on underneath. He had never witnessed such a thing: such simultaneous illumination and translucency of skin, and it was awkward and unfortunate, how they did not fit together as easily and as pleasurably as he had always dreamed, especially now, being newly promised to one another. He held her, forsaking his own desires to soothe her and tell her he would be as patient as she needed him to be.

There in that bed in the cabin in the woods, she told him that she felt very strongly that she was an angel, one of the fallen ones and that the world was nothing but deception to her; all the other earthbound angels were successfully concealing themselves from her in magnificent ways: the paper boy, the pharmacist, the bagger at the supermarket, but their stare lingered a bit too long, enough for her to register confirmation, enough for them to give themselves away. Robert noted the smile on her lips and thought she was saying this in jest; she sometimes had a sarcasm about her, a high-level sarcasm that could be easily misunderstood. God, she said, was concealing Himself from her, because she had not learned what she needed to learn and lived how she needed to live. She needed to accept the earthbound life and live it and love others and give to others and make others happy. "Starting with you," she said to Robert. "Starting with you, because you are good, wholesome and good, through and through and you deserve more than anyone to be happy. So, I will make you happy, and we will do good things together." Only then, she said, would the great revelation occur, after her work had been done, after his work had been done, and the material world would drop away, like petals from a flower.

He had thought it was a lovely metaphor, the angel, the flower, the world falling away, that it was a poetic way to view life and the hereafter. And he imagined them doing wonderful things together, maybe becoming part of a larger group, traveling the world, helping the unfortunate, raising their kids in environments of world outreach and compassion, and being a penetrable force of good. And he would learn from her, revel in her uniqueness and her direct connection to God. She had told him about her fasting, how, after a day without food, she could hear God's voice more clearly. She often spoke passionately about God, like a saint would, in an intimate and personal way, not abstractly, as he had himself perceived God, a being once removed, a being that sat behind a closed door, listening, but never saying anything. He was looking forward to a lifetime of learning from her, of seeing God as a being you could actually communicate with, have a conversation with—the one being who could direct your path in life so that it could reach its full potential and you could reap blessing upon blessing upon blessing. "I know now," she said, "that it all starts with gratitude. From there, anything is possible."

When they pulled her body from the lake, he felt nothing but guilt: it was clear to him, then, that he had downplayed her illness. The weight loss, the dreams of angels, the sudden proposal. Something was awry, something was abnormal, and he convinced himself, successfully, that she was an exceptional person with exceptional intentions. He saw now that the marriage proposal was a last attempt of grounding herself, of living a semi-normal life. Robert blamed himself for not doing the right thing and getting her help, for being selfish and wanting her all to himself. But the mystery of what happened to her is relentless. Just when he believed he had accepted it and moved on, he spirals back to the questioning, the incessant questioning and analysis of what happened and the mystery is present again, in full force, to grapple with. Now there was Nicoletta, her doppelganger. Was he being tested, again, because he had not learned his lesson—to stop putting his selfish desires first, to the disadvantage of another?

After Gregory left, he sat at the wooden table alone and prayed. *Kyrie Eleison, Kyrie Eleison, Christe Eleison.* He prayed for Gregory and any pain he had caused him. He prayed for Elena's soul, and for Nicoletta to be well. He prayed for Florence, who was also dealing with grief. He prayed to accept the mystery, to assimilate it into his life and see it as a gift, a means to exercise faith. This was the essence of it all: faith. He wrestled with his mind, sitting there in the dark, to stay on task, to pray instead of wonder and speculate, to focus on the Virgin, now wearing a cloak of snow.

CHAPTER 8
DANCING ON ROOFTOPS
FLORENCE

Florence made an appointment for ten; this was sufficient time for her to go to morning mass, eat something, and take the bus to Dion's. She looked at herself in the mirror, at the gray marching out of her scalp. Florence wondered if Dante could see her grays, wherever he was. When he was alive, she never let them show because she was always on top of things. Now, a year after his death, she was slipping and the gray and the white wiry hair were becoming apparent at her temples and scalp.

Lately, Florence dreamed of dancing on rooftops. During the day, when she was out hanging clothes or walking to the store, she remembered the dream and the dancing and the sky of stars and the elegant white tablecloths and a faceless partner. The wrinkles and extra pounds, the varicose veins, and the gray and the white wiry hair fell away and she welcomed back her younger body. Dreaming was like going back in time, and it was a welcome escape from the loneliness and limitations of being old.

It must be the spring. This is what she thought to herself, as she hustled to morning mass, remembering that springtime was a time for the ballrooms to open and feature the big bands. Back in the day, she never danced on any rooftops, only in ballrooms like the Arcadia where the Brooklyn boys were fast talkers and could keep a girl light on her feet. Dante never danced, but that didn't matter, because he was overseas at war. Then Dante came home, and they got married. And then the ballrooms closed and the children were born and Dante moved them out to the Island and Florence stared out the kitchen window at a potato farm and wondered what the hell she was doing all the way out there.

Father Crane served the mass and it was always most expedient when he did. As much as she liked Father Kirton, his homilies tended to be long, and half the time she wondered what he was going on and on about. Florence slipped out the door without any of her friends cornering her to talk or ask if she wanted to go for coffee, and made it to the steps before the last hymn was over. She grabbed on to the cold metal railing and eased herself down the stairs, feeling the ache and pain of arthritis in her knees, and was at the bus stop ten minutes later.

It was a sunny, blustering day in April and the clouds were moving fast across the sky, like they had somewhere else they needed to be. The wind was at first refreshing, but then when the clouds covered the morning sun, it became cold, and she wanted desperately for the bus to come. She sat on the bench in the overhang and tried to decipher what play was being advertised with half the poster ripped away by the wind. A car drove by and then stopped, backing up. Father Kirton rolled down the window, "Florence, do you need a ride somewhere?"

It took a moment for Florence to realize who it was in the nondescript car that looked like something an old person might drive. She stood up to look more closely inside and saw that it was Father Kirton, with a scarf wrapped around his neck. She went toward the door and opened it and sat in the car, with the heat blasting out toward the seats.

"Where can I take you?" Father Kirton asked.

"Oh I'm just going to Dion's down past the library on Pulaski Road. I would walk it, but my legs are bothering me this morning. Arthritis in my knees."

"Well, I'll get you there in a jiffy," Kirton said.

"Thank you, Father. I really don't mind taking the bus, but the wind, this morning—"

"Yes, the wind is terrible this morning. Frustrating time of year. We all just want it to be warm."

Father Kirton put on his blinker and carefully pulled out on to the road.

"This is the time of year my husband and I would go to Florida. It's beautiful down there now."

"Are you not going to go this year?" Father Kirton asked, maneuvering the lights on Larkfield Road and the people on the cross walk, and the cars changing lanes. He stopped at a red light and Florence observed how the lights were dancing while hanging from their wires.

"I don't know. It seems more of hassle when it's just me."

Florence felt the warm air from the vent hit her knees and it felt good. She noted how the car was immaculate, and seemed more like a rental than a car someone owned. They reached the salon, and Father Kirton got out of the car to open Florence's door for her to help her out. This is something Dante always did as well, because it was tricky to get in and out of cars with the arthritis. Father Kirton told her he had a few errands to do, and if he saw her out at the bus stop near Dion's when he returned, he'd fetch her then too. Florence thanked him kindly and went into the salon, thinking it was a long shot that she would run into him again, but when she was done, he was actually out front waiting for her. Florence's hair was now an auburn color and blown in a bouffant wave off her head. There were slight smears of auburn coloring near her ears.

"Father, were you waiting here the entire time?"

"Oh no, no. Just got here. I had to get the car inspected and then have the tires rotated. I've only been here a minute or two. How about we go to the Larkfield Depot for lunch? My treat."

"Oh, you don't have to do that, Father. I have food to eat at home."

"I would like to do it. In fact, I insist."

Florence smiled. "Well, if you insist," she said. "A bowl of soup would be nice."

*

When Father Kirton dropped Florence off at the hairdresser, he knew he was going to ask her to go to lunch with him upon picking her up. He questioned his motive, whether it was to truly help Florence, or to find out about Nicoletta. But he sensed that Florence was a bit depressed, that something was bothering her, because lately she'd been quiet and a bit withdrawn when he was in her company. This was something he was attuned to in people.

They looked at the choices on the Larkfield Depot menu and Florence remembered how she and Dante would come here sometimes after going for a walk on the beach, and Dante would call the waitresses by their first names, as if he'd known them for years. This was something Dante always did when they went out to eat—joke and become chummy with the waitresses. He liked to order the eggs benedict, even though his cholesterol tended to be high. "Once in a while," he'd tell Florence. "Once in a while, I'll have the eggs benny. That's all. Everyone needs to live a little, even if they're old." And she chuckled to herself about how he said that every time they came here. And how he enjoyed every bit of the eggs benedict and left nothing on the plate.

"I've been praying for you, Father," she said suddenly, trying to jar her mind from going down its path of memory.

"And I you," Kirton said. "But I can't help but think it's not being effective."

"Of course it is, Father! Why would you say that?"

"No, no, I mean. Right. Of course it's effective in ways I can't see, but something seems to be wrong, Florence. You seem quiet, as if something is bothering you."

Florence was surprised that someone noticed. She looked at Father Kirton with his scarf still tucked around his neck and his hair mussed from the wind; at his handsome face with the movie-star jawline and seraphic eyes. "It's the spring," she said. "You're expected to be happy in the spring. I thought I'd get my hair done, because that's what I've always done, but really, I don't care one way or another."

"I think it's grief, Florence."

Florence looked at the old men at the counter, eating their donuts, talking with the waitresses, how they've figured it out, to get themselves out the door, talk to people, keep at it, no matter what. She wondered if Dante would have been one of those men as well, if it were she who died. She felt a pinch come to her nose and her eyes well up.

"He kept track of me, Father. He always noticed when I had my hair done. He noticed the new dresses, the new coats, the new pocketbooks. This made me feel good. Now there is no one to keep track of me, and I feel invisible. What does it matter if I sit at the kitchen table with a cup of coffee in the morning or not? I might as well stay in bed all day. No one would notice."

"I would notice, Florence. The women in the Legion would notice."

"You're sweet, Father," Florence, said, dabbing her eyes.

The waitress came and they both ordered Manhattan clam chowder and a cup of coffee. The waitress took their menus, and Florence continued to talk, feeling like it was okay, and noting to herself that she would not mention how she thought Dante was visiting her and slapping her behind, no matter how comfortable she became with the conversation, for fear that the priest would think she was losing her mind.

"In spring, he would look forward to playing golf. It was good to go our separate ways for the day and then come back together in the evening, have dinner, and he'd tell me about his day and all of the little things he observed about people, their funny habits. Like how one of his buddies used to stick out his tongue whenever he hit a putt. "Again with the tongue," he'd say, and we would have a chuckle. We were company for one another after all those years of marriage. How hard it was to live with him sometimes, with his anxieties about the kids, and his lack of faith. We finally settled into this—comfort—we had finally grown in harmony with one another and it was a beautiful thing, and I don't know how to be in harmony without him. I do things. I try, but the harmony is not there. The harmony with life, that is."

Father Kirton listened to Florence, as she talked about her grief and dabbed at her eyes with a crumpled tissue from her purse, and thought to himself how the only time he felt harmony with life was when he was alone, walking the beach, or alone, walking in the woods or at mass, when someone else was serving it. His harmony had nothing to do with another person, and he realized then, that maybe the grief he had known was only an inkling of what it could have been, if he had lived out a life with Elena. But grieving over a missed opportunity was not the same as grieving over the loss of a true beloved. He reached over and grasped Florence's cold, arthritic hands and held them in his own.

The waitress came by with two steaming bowls and two steaming cups, and he relinquished Florence's hands, embarrassed almost, and the two sat back in the seats of the booth. The waitress placed the two cups of Manhattan clam chowder in front of them and the coffees as well, taking care not to spill a drop, and Kirton was surprised at how quickly Florence could conceal her tears and upgrade her voice to something worthy of public discourse without any indication of emotional upheaval. It was a quick switch on, then off.

The two shared a cup of soup and Kirton thought it better not to lecture Florence on the sorrows and glories of the Lord, that just listening to her was enough for today, because today, she needed to tell someone the story of how she met Dante Alighieri Russo and how he changed her life.

It was Florence's mother who got them together, because she wanted Florence out of the house and one less mouth to feed. She was the second oldest of the four girls and she was beautiful; Philomena figured it would be easy to marry her off first. But Florence was picky when it came to suitors and she had designs of her own. She liked to go dancing at the Arcadia, the Million Dollar Ballroom, where there were swing bands, and the fellas were sharp dressers and good dancers. She had her eye on a young man named Walter Pogee; he was tall with broad shoulders, blond hair, and eyes impeccably blue, like yours, Father, just like yours, Florence said, blue like some magnificent gem, so unlike the coal dark eyes of her siblings and parents. All of Walter's family was good-looking; Florence would see them at church and his mother and sisters always wore fashionable hats and suits. Walter's mother looked like the actress Loretta Young and his sister won the Rockaway beauty contest. She thought that it would be a privilege to be a part of that family.

Florence was insulted by the fact that her mother wanted to set her up with the butcher's nephew. The butcher shop was underneath the El where the old men played bocci ball and whistled at the young women walking by, "*Hey dollee, what do you say, dollee?*" Some of them were old enough to be her father. What had gotten into her mother that she wanted to fix her up with a guy from that place? They were the ones who got the girls in trouble. Florence remembered then what her mother used to tell her and her sisters, and she did not tell Father Kirton this: "You go with men like that and *sall a ves!*" her mother would say, dialect for how she'd salt their private places so they wouldn't come home with a belly and yet another mouth to feed. But Pop was always there to defend his daughters. "*Dona talk a like that!*" he'd say. "*These are a my girls and they are a good girls!*"

She told him that as a girl, she hid in the front room behind the French doors where her grandmother slept when she was alive. It smelled like camphor and had pictures of relatives in the old country and was decorated with statues and paintings of baby angels. It was the perfect place to hide and weep, because she felt her mother didn't love her. Florence was a lonely child; her three sisters didn't pay much attention to her. Mary had a big mouth and was always arguing with Philomena and Jenny and Edith had each other and often didn't include her. Her older brother was overseas in the military and the younger brother was too young to be company. It was difficult to be a child with a mother who ignored you. In her loneliness, she prayed to Mother Cabrini, the immigrant saint. In the fall when the afternoon light shone through the window and highlighted the cross on her grandmother's dresser, she felt as if the saint was in the room, comforting her. She conversed with the saint and told her the sorrows that plagued her heart and sometimes, when she did this, the sun shone directly on her, evidence that Mother Cabrini was listening.

Florence dug into her purse and took out a picture of Mother Cabrini and showed it to Father Kirton.

When her mother came home late from work and her father had nothing to eat, he would yell at her and make little Sandro cry. Florence's sisters would get between them and cajole him, boiling the water for the pasta and serving it with olive oil and garlic, because there was no more sauce left over from Sunday. Amidst the chaos, Florence would fetch the picture and set it under the lamp and she felt as if the saint were whispering straight to her heart, easing her worries. Her father didn't mean to be violent; it was the wine and the darkness. It would all be better in the morning when he would wear his white button-down shirt with the tape measure around his neck and sit at the table for his eggs and bacon with little Sandro on his knee. She kissed the picture and told her baby brother to kiss it too, if he was with her, to soothe him as well.

The summer months were always happier, when relatives would gather in the backyard and they would all eat at a long table under the grapevines. Pop would grow a garden and have sunflowers and tomatoes and hot peppers. Pop was happiest during the warmer months when Valentino was home from the military with gifts from the world—a cuckoo clock from the Black Forest, a wooden chest with carved dragons from China, tiny metal goblets from Venice for sambuca—and the vines were ripe with grapes for making wine. The long table was moved inside for the holidays with the smoke of Pop's cigar crowding the room and the animated stories Valentino would tell and everyone would laugh.

As she grew older, Florence became close with her brother Sandro who had the same shy demeanor. The two would escape to the Strand on Queens Boulevard to watch movies with Fred Astaire and Rita Hayworth. Florence thought Rita was a good model on how a woman should be, how she should dress, what she should say to be alluring but classy. Rita Hayworth was everything her mother was not.

Philomena became impatient with Florence and insisted that she go buy the week's meat at the butcher and give the butcher's nephew a chance. Florence wasn't one to argue with her mother and bring on her wrath like her sister Mary did. She appeased her and went to the store.

Dante was taller than the men in her family. He had a thin mustache like the gangsters wore. She did not admit to herself that he was good-looking. While she waited in line she watched and listened as he spoke Italian to the old women and was very polite with all of the customers, *Va bene, Signorina, grazie Signorina.* It was a hot day in July when the city streets radiated with heat; a fan whirred in the shop near the ice box, blowing the cool air over the counter. When she placed her order, he asked her if she was from around here, how he never saw her before. She told him she had to shop for her mother, because she wasn't feeling well, that her mother was Philomena Calabrese, and she usually came late, after work. Dante told Florence he remembered her mother, that she was a woman you don't forget; a woman who doesn't take no for an answer. Florence liked the way a dark piece of hair fell over his eyes.

When she went home, Philomena asked her about Dante and Florence said that he wasn't her type.

"Flo is sweet on Walter Pogee," Mary said with her big mouth.

"Bahhh," Philomena said, waving her hand at Florence. "*He's a fulla himself,*" she said.

Florence started making trips to Liberty Avenue to the soda shop where Walter and his chums hung out. Dante used to watch her pass his store, on the way there. She wore a new sundress she had made from a pair of curtains.

"Where you going all dressed up like that?" Dante asked her. "You got a fella?"

"Maybe I do," Florence said.

"Whoever he is, forget him. Let's go have dinner tonight in Astoria."

Florence thought for a moment. She would love to get away from her crowded house to eat in a nice restaurant in Astoria, but she didn't want to give Dante the wrong idea.

"I can't. I'm busy."

"Oh yeah? What are you doing?"

"None of your business."

Dante didn't give up easy. The next day when he saw her heading for Liberty Avenue, he closed shop early and followed her. The goons playing bocci underneath the El betrayed him, "Hey Dante! Hey, what do you say Dante?" Florence turned around, and Dante stopped and pretended he was reading the paper he brought as a prop.

"Listen," she said, walking up to him, "Leave me alone. I gotta meet somebody."

"Who?"

"None of your business. Who do you think you are following me around like this?"

"What are you afraid of? I don't mean anybody any harm. I just want to talk, that's all."

The El rattled and thundered by and Florence walked away, not looking back.

Florence would stop by the soda shop on a daily basis to see if Walter was there with the fellas he hung around with. When he was there, she watched him from the window, noting what he was wearing, how well his clothes fit him, how he kept his cool in conversation and did not over gesticulate like most of the people in her neighborhood. She fumbled with her purse, made it look like she was waiting for the bus and searching for change, all the while trying to work up the nerve to go in and order a milkshake and ask Walter if he was going to the Arcadia Million Dollar Ballroom Saturday night. But it all seemed impossible, opening the door and walking up to the counter, using her voice to ask for something and inquiring of Walter of his plans. It was much easier to remain unnoticed. So, Florence continued to admire Walter from afar, waiting for fate to miraculously bring them together.

Florence decided to sew Rita Hayworth's champagne-colored gown with the flower decals from *You Were Never Lovelier*. It was a difficult project and took months to sew. The chiffon in the catalogue was too expensive, so she used the scraps from her mother's bridal gown alterations. She planned to have the gown finished for the appearance of the Tommy Dorsey Band at the Arcadia in two weeks. In the evening, after her parents and sisters left the shop, she stayed working on the gown, carefully pinning it to the pattern, sewing the hems on her mother's old Singer. She meticulously sewed each decal by hand. Once the bodice and skirt were in place, she tried the gown on, and admired herself in the mirror.

Outside, the darkness hid the detritus of the city; the lights from the buildings and how they shone on the wet streets made the city look elegant and mysterious. Across the river, skyscrapers disappeared into mist, and somewhere men were wearing coats and tails with pressed shirts and women wore gowns that flowed around their bodies like water. Somewhere champagne was poured into fluted glasses and there were chandeliers that did dazzling things with light.

Sandro had a shoe shine business outside his father's tailor shop, catering to the Jewish businessmen who went into the city. He watched her from behind the door, waiting to walk her home. She talked to the mirror as if it were Walter; she rehearsed the lines she would say to him. Sandro cat-called and startled her.

"How long have you been standing there?"

"Long enough."

"I'll be ready to go in a minute."

He went to his sister and grabbed her hand. He was now Florence's height and she noticed how his jaw was becoming more prominent; the bones were stretching his boy face into a man's. He had Pop's brow, eyes, and nose, a face that had a history on another continent. His body was long and lithe, but strong. He could now effectively subdue his father when he had too much wine. Florence inhaled Sandro's scent when he came close, a mixture of soap and leather. Sandro put on the radio and the two danced in the shop, laughing and pretending they were on the set of a movie. When the music stopped, Sandro looked at his sister. "If I weren't your brother, Flo, I'd want you for my girl," he said.

When they arrived home, the girls were whispering in the bedroom. Philomena was pregnant again and she wanted Mary to take her to a doctor in the "back alley." Mary thought it was the right thing to do. She had known some seamstresses from Manhattan who had gone to him, and he was professional and clean.

"Momma's too old to have another. And besides, it might not come out right: something will be wrong with it."

"Maybe if she waits awhile it will bleed out. That's what happened to Dilly's mother. They don't stay in when the mother is old."

All of this talk made Florence feel anxious. She didn't want anything to do with her mother's problem; it was a sin if she got rid of the baby. If anyone found out, her mother would be banned from the church. She would bring shame to the entire family.

"What do you think, Jenny?" asked Mary.

"I think if you don't take her, she'll dig it out herself with whatever she can find," said Jenny.

Sandro and Florence went to see a new movie called *Casablanca*. Florence wasn't interested in it, because it wasn't a musical with her beloved Fred Astaire and Rita Hayworth, but she wanted to get out of the house. They bought popcorn and Coca-Cola and settled in and before the movie started, Florence noticed a man sitting a few rows ahead of them. By the silhouette of his head, it could've been Walter. She thought if she wished hard enough, it might turn out to be him. She prayed to Mother Cabrini to please let it be him. When the lights came on, the man got up, and Florence gathered her coat and purse, grabbed Sandro's arm, and pushed her way through the crowd, before fear took hold of her. The doors burst open into the cold night air, everywhere was the sound of heels on concrete. She saw the man under the street lamp and charged after him, despite the feeling of knowing something was off. When she reached him, he turned around as if he knew she was coming and as he did, Florence was face to face with Dante Alighieri Russo.

"It's you," she said.

"Of course it's me," he said, "Who else would it be?"

Florence grabbed Sandro's arm to go.

"Wait, wait," he said standing in front of them. "Did you like the movie? That guy Bogart sure is swell."

"I think he's got a mug like a dog," Florence said.

"What do you think, kid?" Dante smiled. He put out his hand and Sandro took it. "What's your name, kid?"

"Sandro."

"A good name from the old country. How old are you?"

"Fourteen."

"Do you look after your mother?"

Sandro nodded his head.

"My mother doesn't need anyone to take care of her," Florence said.

Dante struck up a conversation with Sandro to keep Florence from leaving. He took them both to the soda shop and bought them ice cream. When Florence ordered a vanilla shake, Dante ordered one as well. "See that, the whole world likes chocolate and you and me like vanilla," he said. "That's something, isn't it?"

In the bright light of the soda shop, Florence noticed Dante's jet-black hair, it was the blackest hair she had ever seen and it had a beautiful shine to it. Dante smoked and talked to everyone around him. He was on a first name basis with the soda man and cracked jokes with him. Florence realized then that he wasn't like the fellas at the dance hall, or even Walter for the matter. He seemed older, and his quick-witted confidence was appealing. Florence looked down at the table and didn't talk much. She was worried Walter would come in and see her with Dante; she was also worried about Sandro, who was tired from waking up at dawn all week long and whose circles under his eyes looked darker. She drank half her shake and stood up. Dante stood up as well.

"Thank you," she said to Dante, "I'm tired and want to go home. I have to work tomorrow."

She was surprised at the way she voiced her desire, with confidence.

"I'll walk you home," Dante said.

They talked about the Arcadia and the Tommy Dorsey Band and how they would be playing tomorrow night. Sandro told Dante he should go, and Dante said he didn't dance, but he'd go for the music. Florence was taken aback that this arrangement took place without her say, and she was beginning to feel conflicted about whether she wanted him around or not.

When Sandro and Florence returned home, their parents were arguing in the kitchen. Jenny, Mary, and Edith were playing cards in the dining room, waiting out their father's fury.

"He knows something," Jenny said.

"What's done is done," Mary said.

Sandro stayed in the kitchen and attempted to quell the fight, while Florence went up to her room. She sat on the bed, and looked at the dress hanging on the closet door; her entire body reverberated with excitement and anticipation. The argument continued until there was a crash that came from downstairs. One of her sisters screamed. When she reached the kitchen, her mother was cradling Sandro's head in her hands, smacking his face. "Wake up! Wake up!" she shouted.

"What happened!"

"He slipped," Mary said. "It's nothing, he just slipped."

"He hit his head and it knocked him out," Jenny said.

"You pushed him, Pop! Why did you do that!" Edith yelled.

"Did you push him?" Florence asked.

"*I jus pussha him outta the way!*" Pop said. "*He getta in my face. Thinks I'm gonna hurt his a mother! I dona hurt her! We yell, but I dona hurt her!*" he said.

Sandro came to and rose slowly. "I'm awake, I'm awake! Stop slapping me!"

"*You putta ice on it. Putta ice on it,*" Pop said.

"Alright, alright," Sandro said, waving him away.

Pop went into the den to smoke a cigar, drink more of his wine, and listen to the radio, while Philomena wrapped a dish towel in ice and applied it to Sandro's head. Florence went up to bed, her hopes deflated about life being any different from what it was.

The night Florence and her sisters went to the Million Dollar Ballroom, Florence had the premonition that something wonderful was about to happen. It wasn't just the excitement of the impending night; it was something else, something to do with fate and how she wouldn't have to do much to make it all happen.

Florence borrowed Mary's T-strap shoes and Mary borrowed Edith's pillbox hat and Edith wore Jenny's long satin gloves. The girls mixed and matched with exuberance and complimented one another on what looked best on whom. Philomena was downstairs playing cards with the neighbor women, reminiscing about the mountain villages in Calabria and what herbs they grew. The girls left in a flurry to catch the A-train, planning to meet Mary's seamstress friends in the city at a diner close to the ballroom. It was early spring and the sun, growing in its strength had melted all the snow, save the dirty piles in the shadows of the El. When they met Dilly and Katherine, who sat in a booth smoking cigarettes and drinking black coffee, Dilly said Flo should be onstage with the Rockettes with a dress like that. Flo scoffed at the idea and said she was too short. Dilly told Florence that Walter was sure to be there tonight, and that she would introduce him, and she snapped her gum and winked at her when she said this. Florence was embarrassed that Mary opened her big mouth again about Walter, but she was happy too, that finally, the link between them had materialized. Things were beginning to fall into place.

When the girls checked their coats and headed for the ballroom, Sandro flashed across Florence's mind; she wondered if he and his friends would show up, sneak in through the janitor's door, like they did before, and dance with the older girls. The band was just warming up and stray notes and trills of the horns and the powdered thump of the bass drum could be heard intermittently. The musicians were debonair and cool, dressed in their white suits, and Florence liked to watch them as they played, wondering what it would be like to have a talent like that, to be able to make music that everyone loved.

When the lights dimmed, and the music began, Walter showed up with his chums and they sat in the next table over. Florence's face went hot and she felt weak in the knees, she sat down at the table with her sisters and took a long sip of Mary's gin and tonic. Dilly went over to Walter and shouted in his ear. Florence stared at the magnificent chandelier in the middle of the ballroom, at the thousand points of light. She told herself to breathe. Some fellas came over and asked the girls to dance and Florence turned them down, she rushed to the powder room to put on some lipstick and gather herself. On the way there she passed by a man sitting alone at a table, smoking a cigar. It was Dante. He waved, and she ducked into the powder room. She spritzed her wrist with perfume and reapplied her lipstick, told herself as long as she kept to the dance floor, he wouldn't go near her, since he didn't dance. There was a black woman sitting in the corner selling feminine napkins and wet wipes. She immediately tuned into Florence's anxiety.

"Girl, you gotta get out there and knock 'em dead! Oooooweeeee! Look at that dress!"

Florence told her she made it herself.

"Talented and beautiful! You one lucky girl!" It was a compliment that fortified her, and when women poured into the powder room, Florence went out, toward the dance floor and ran straight into Walter, who smiled and took her hand.

They immediately fell into dancing as the horns erupted with sound and the bass kept the melody. Florence never felt more alive, dancing with Walter; in this moment, she was exactly who she wanted to be and the world fell away from her. When she looked toward the table where Dante sat, he was gone.

It was strange, however, that Walter hardly spoke to her. In fact, she couldn't remember the sound of his voice, later, taking the train home. When she tried to recall it, all she could hear was Dante's voice, his confident, clear voice in her ear. She closed her eyes and tried desperately to remember Walter's voice, as she lived the moment over again and again in her mind, the warmth of Walter's hand, how he instinctively knew how to lead her, how he smelled like licorice and oranges and how wonderful it was to move effortlessly with him. But it was all over in a flash, despite dancing all night, and Florence was aglow in her own euphoria, confident that Walter would call on her the next day.

When they got home it was late, but all of the lights were on in the house, which the girls thought strange, because Pop always went around shutting them off to save money on the electric bill. They came in quietly through the kitchen where there was mud on the floor, and someone was weeping and speaking in Italian. They looked at one another with apprehension and went to the living room where Philomena sat holding the hands of the neighbor women. Pop was at the back of the room, staring out the window. When the girls entered, Philomena collapsed on the floor and wailed, "My boy! My boy! He a no wake up! He a no wake up!"

Philomena sat weeping in the front room most of the night, praying for Sandro to open his eyes, even after the doctor pronounced him dead at 9:05 PM the previous night. Florence and her sisters listened to the weeping and the pleas with God until Philomena eventually fell asleep and nothing could be heard but the rain hitting the roof and Pop wandering the halls, muttering to himself, drunk. Florence's mind was flooded with memories of Sandro and how wonderfully alive he was only two days ago. Her mind grappled with the idea of Sandro's permanent absence from her life. She would get married, have children, grow old, Sandro would forever remain a young man. She felt abandoned, alone, and terrified that God's wrath enacted such a swift and severe punishment to the family.

The next day, the neighbor women came with hams and breads and long pans of lasagna and stuffed shells. They dressed Sandro in the same gallant suit Pop made for him for his confirmation and filled the coffin with silk flowers. Florence stayed away from the preparations, and kept to herself in her room. When the viewing officially started, Florence locked herself in her room. The next morning, when it came time to close the coffin and carry it to church for the funeral, Florence put on her coat, passed the mourners and sequestered herself to the backyard, waiting for the coffin to be carried out. She huddled under the grapevines; tiny leaves were now appearing on the wood. After a few minutes the screen door slammed and she looked up and there was Dante. He descended the steps and approached her slowly, as if she were a feral animal.

"Florence," he said. "They are going to close the casket. I will go with you. I will go with you to kneel and say a prayer. It's the right thing to do."

Dante put his arm around her, and she could feel the life force coming off him, the warmth of someone alive. They walked slowly up the stairs and into the house.

"You'll see, Florence. It's just like he's sleeping. He's one of the good ones—I could just tell—and they don't last long here, in our world. But he's gone now to a better place, a place where he belongs, and it's okay."

They stopped at the portal to the front room and Florence looked in and saw Sandro tucked amongst the silk flowers, small, and sleeping serenely. She felt fortified by having Dante walk with her, so she went to the coffin and wept. Dante held her hand. He bowed his head and said a prayer. Then he rose and kissed the boy on the top of his head.

The priest asked the family to convene around the coffin and Dante stayed with Florence to hear the prayer being said for Sandro's soul. She was exhausted. But what Dante said made sense. And when her own son was born dead, the umbilical cord wrapped tightly about his neck and body, she thought about what Dante said again, that this world wasn't fit for some souls, and that we should see it as Dante did, that it was a privilege just to love them during the short time they were here.

Father Kirton nodded his head in agreement.

Florence thanked Father Kirton for listening to her story. She told him she felt much better, but she needed to go home and take a nap; her son was coming for dinner and she wanted to rest before she had to prepare the meal. Kirton paid for the soup and coffee and helped Florence with her coat. When they exited the restaurant, the sun was shining and the wind died down, and the day was warm with promise—a promise that only the spring can bring. Father Kirton drove Florence home and once again, opened her door for her.

"You're spoiling me, Father," she said and shooed him away when he tried to help her up her own stairs.

When he saw that she was safe and inside, he went back to his car, exited the driveway, drove twenty-five feet, and turned into the rectory parking lot. He shut the engine off and sat for a moment, noting how he felt settled inside. *Only in hindsight can we see how the pieces fit together,* he thought to himself. He felt a glow of appreciation for his own life. Father Kirton went up the rectory steps, feeling inspired to get it all down. To write—.

EPILOGUE

Florence was slicing the bread for the meal when she heard a knock at the door. She walked hastily across the kitchen floor, excited about having a guest for dinner.

"Oh, it's you!" she said, touching her chest lightly, as her husband strolled in wearing his yellow and blue plaid golf pants, softly whistling to himself. Florence shut the door and followed him into the kitchen.

"I'm so glad you decided to come," she said, feeling the back of her coiffed hair. She fetched the carafe of Gallo Paisano wine from the counter and poured a glass for her guest and then poured herself some. "Bardo bought the wine. He finally got the kind I like."

Sounds of trucks, car alarms, far away sirens, peppered in with the early spring air through an open window.

"Here, have some Italian bread to hold you while we wait for the pasta fagiole," she said, nudging the basket toward her husband. "Come on now. Take a slice. It's delicious. Baked today. When I bought the bag, it was still warm." She went to the stove to turn down the heat on the soup.

"Did I tell you that Edith and Jenny are going to visit Valentino next week in Palm Beach? They asked me to go. I remember when you and me used to go. They tell me to go, but I don't know. "

He placed his hands behind his head just like he used to when he listened to her stories.

"I saw Chet the other day at Bohack's. He's getting fat. Said his back has been bothering him. That's why he's not playing golf. But really, I think it's because he misses you." She bent down to check on the ribs in the broiler. "I think they are done," she said. She pulled the ribs from the broiler and put them in a dish. "Look at that, perfectly done," she said. She then doled out the soup in the bowls, placed them on the table, and sat down. She passed the parmesan cheese toward Dante. "Here, I got this from the deli. They grate it right in front of you, if you ask them to."

Dante sprinkled some cheese on his soup and tasted a spoonful.

"And Nicoletta is doing very well at her job. She got a raise and is going to go to school to be a paralegal. She seems different now, more confident. The lawyer she works with said he would help her with the classes."

They drank the wine and finished the soup and then ate the ribs and Florence talked and talked, about the family and her president and the Marion Legion and she was so busy talking, she wasn't watching what she was doing and spilled wine on her shirt.

"Oh, will you look at that! Just my dumb luck! I only bought this shirt last week!"

She immediately fetched a bottle of seltzer from the fridge and dabbed the stain at the sink, but it didn't come out.

"I'm going up to change and put this shirt in the wash."

Florence went upstairs and removed the shirt, tossed it into the hamper. Downstairs, the stereo played the signature first lines of *In the Mood*. Her heart swelled as the music filled the house. She went to the closet, sifted through her wardrobe, picked out the chiffon gown she wore ten years ago to her niece's wedding and laid it carefully on the bed. She put on her stockings, her heels, the dress, dabbed her wrists with perfume. She grabbed a lipstick from the dresser and stared deeply into the mists. Before she outlined her lips, she noticed something was different; it was her face.

"Well, I'll be darned," she said.

When she descended the stairs, Dante was standing in the middle of the living room, fixing the cufflinks on his sleeve. He reached out his hand to her, and she smirked.

"Who you kiddin'" Dante, you don't dance."

"I do now, Florence," he said.

Acknowledgments

I am indebted to my manuscript readers Anne Marie La Bue, Erin Miller, Andrea Tupper, Jane Mosco, and Diana Lynch for their insightful feedback and taking time out of their hectic lives to read drafts of the book. I am grateful for the support and platform of the Italian American Writers Association (IAWA), especially Julia Lisella and Jennifer Martelli, who put time and effort into creating a welcoming community where writers can share their work. Every writer needs a community to call home, and I've finally found mine. Many thanks to Nicola Orichuia of IAM Books in the North End where most of the IAWA gatherings happen: if it weren't for you, this community would not have gathered. Thank you for your unflinching support of the Italian diaspora. Special thanks goes out to Nic Grosso for his dedication in producing quality texts at Bordighera, to Catherine Parnell (as always) for her impeccable eye, and Olivia Kate Cerrone for her support.

The following texts were extremely helpful in crafting the character Father Robert Kirton: Thomas Merton's *The Seven Story Mountain*, Dr. (Father) Capuchin Zeno's biography of John Henry Newman, titled *John Henry Newman, His Inner Life*, and St. Augustine's *Confessions*.

My research into the vodou (voo doo) religion spanned decades from when I wrote the first draft in the early nineties to the most recent drafts in 2024. Vodou terminology spellings varies from text to text, and I didn't hold allegiance to any one, because there seems to be no particular standard. A very good source on vodou, especially with respect to the personalities of the lwas (spirits) is Bob Corbett's site: faculty.webster.edu/corbetre/haiti/voodoo/voodoo.htm. Also, Wade Davis's article in Harper's Magazine titled "The Pharmacology of Zombies" was conveniently informative with respect to the use of tetrodotoxin in vodou culture and helped in writing Sabine's encounter with the vodouisant. Lastly, I found inspiration in Marie Vieux-Chauvet's wonderful Haitian Trilogy *Love, Anger, Madness*.

About the Author

LAURETTE FOLK's fiction, essays, and poems have been published in *Waxwing, Gravel, Brilliant Flash Fiction, Boston Globe Magazine,* and *Best Small Fictions.* Her first novel, *A Portal to Vibrancy,* won the Independent Press Award for New Adult Fiction. Her second novel, *The End of Aphrodite,* won the Eric Hoffer Award for General Fiction and wais described by Kirkus Reviews as "[a] haunting and poignant reflection on grief, spirituality, and the loving bonds that provide guidance and sustenance." Laurette is a Pushcart Prize and Best of the Net nominee and a graduate of the Vermont College MFA in Writing program.

VIA Folios

A refereed book series dedicated to the culture of Italians and Italian Americans.

HELEN BAROLINI. *Chiaroscuro: Essays of Identity*. Vol 11. Essays.

PICARAZZI & FEINSTEIN, Eds. *An African Harlequin in Milan*. Vol 10. Theater/Essays.

JOSEPH RICAPITO. *Florentine Streets & Other Poems*. Vol 9. Poetry.

FRED MISURELLA. *Short Time*. Vol 8. Novella.

NED CONDINI. *Quartettsatz*. Vol 7. Poetry.

ANTHONY JULIAN TAMBURRI, Ed. *Fuori: Essays by Italian/American Lesbiansand Gays*. Vol 6. Essays.

ANTONIO GRAMSCI. P. Verdicchio. Trans. & Intro. *The Southern Question*. Vol 5. Social Criticism.

DANIELA GIOSEFFI. *Word Wounds & Water Flowers*. Vol 4. Poetry. $8

WILEY FEINSTEIN. *Humility's Deceit: Calvino Reading Ariosto Reading Calvino*. Vol 3. Criticism.

PAOLO A. GIORDANO, Ed. *Joseph Tusiani: Poet. Translator. Humanist*. Vol 2. Criticism.

ROBERT VISCUSI. *Oration Upon the Most Recent Death of Christopher Columbus*. Vol 1. Poetry.

www.ingramcontent.com/pod-product-compliance
Lightning Source LLC
Chambersburg PA
CBHW032009010726
47493CB00007B/2329